Libby faces the most difficult decision of her life.

Spencer's lips touched her brow, her temple, her cheek, leaving warmth in their path. When they reached her lips again, it was many minutes before he released hers.

"I came back to River's Edge because of you, Libby."

Her heart stopped, then barreled on again. "You did?"

"I'd hoped for a glimpse of you, or news of you, at least. When I heard of your husband's death. . . I'm truly sorry for your loss, but, forgive me, when I heard you were a widow, my heart near leaped from my chest in hope."

She held her breath, waiting for him to continue.

"We've lived more years than we're likely to see again." His arms tightened about her. He rubbed his cheek against her hair, almost dislodging her hat. She didn't mind—enjoyed the closeness. "I've lived without you for thirty-five years. I don't intend to spend the rest of my life without you."

Surely he couldn't be proposing after such short reacquaintance! Libby licked her suddenly dry lips. "What. . .what do you mean?"

His chest moved with his soft chuckle. "Is my intention so obscure? I intend to marry you, Libby."

JOANN A. GROTE returns to the Minnesota setting where she herself grew up to set up her own housekeeping and create new, fascinating characters. Like her characters, JoAnn seeks to serve Christ in her work. She believes that readers of novels can receive a message of salvation and encouragement from well-crafted fiction.

Books by JoAnn A. Grote

HEARTSONG PRESENTS
HP36—The Sure Promise
HP51—The Unfolding Heart
HP55—Treasure of the Heart
HP103—Love's Shining Hope
HP120—An Honest Love
HP136—Rekindled Flame
HP184—Hope That Sings
HP288—Sweet Surrender

A Man
for Libby

JoAnn A. Grote

Heartsong Presents

A note from the author:
I love to hear from my readers! You may correspond with me
by writing: **JoAnn A. Grote**
                                      Author Relations
                                      PO Box 719
                                      Uhrichsville, OH 44683

ISBN 1-57748-552-1

A MAN FOR LIBBY

Cover illustration by Lauraine Bush.

PRINTED IN THE U.S.A.

one

River's Edge, Minnesota, 1895

"Look, Evan!" Effie squealed. "This hat would make a great disguise."

Libby Ward chuckled as she watched the eight-year-old girl settle a black hat over her thick, chestnut-brown hair and pull the black net down past her round, freckled face.

"See?"

A boy, who looked identical but with short hair, nodded. "It's perfect for a detective, Effie."

Libby exchanged an amused look with her niece, Constance.

Constance shook her head. "The Troublesome Twins are in their usual form." She walked briskly across Libby's millinery shop, plucked the hat from Effie's head, and set it back on its black cast-iron display stand. "You know Aunt Libby's hats aren't toys. If you must try on hats, look at the children's display. You both need new spring hats."

"It's too nice out in the spring to wear hats," Evan protested.

Effie ignored her aunt's comment entirely. She reached across the table and fingered the delicate black veil. "Did you ever wear a hat like this when you were a Pinkerton detective, Aunt Constance?"

Constance hesitated before replying. "Yes, I'm afraid I did."

Libby grinned. Constance's tone indicated she regretted the truth. She knew Constance was afraid her answer would only encourage the children's already overdeveloped interest in detective work.

"To hide your face from criminals, right?" Effie lifted the hat from its display once more. "Will you buy me one?"

"No." Constance retrieved the hat and replaced it again. "You don't need a mourning hat."

"But how can Evan and me be good detectives without disguises?"

"You've done all too well so far without them. Go look at the children's displays." Constance returned to Libby, looking heavenward. "I fear Justin and I will never cure these two of their infatuation with detective work," she confided when she reached Libby's side.

"I'm sure they'll outgrow it before long."

"Before they are harmed by it, I hope."

The children did have a knack for winding up in the middle of dangerous criminal situations, partly because of Constance's former occupation as a Pinkerton, but Libby tried to reassure her. "It's a small town. There's little crime here."

"Try this one on her." Evan's suggestion was followed by a riot of giggles.

Libby's gaze darted toward the children. Effie was stuffing her most expensive French bonnet onto one-year-old Maria Louise's head. Though it was far too large, the eight-year-old girl was pushing either side of the brim, making certain the bonnet fit as tightly as possible.

"Stop, Effie!" Libby lifted her skirts and started to the hat's rescue. Her heels clicked across the wooden floor as rapidly as a Spanish dancer's staccato.

Effie looked up, her brown eyes wide with innocence beneath her thick brown bangs. Her hands still clutched the hat's brim. "What's wrong, Aunt Libby?"

"What's wrong?" Evan echoed.

Libby propped bony fists on her skinny hips. "You know better than to treat my hats that way."

"Children, apologize to Aunt Libby, right now," Constance demanded.

Evan looked at his feet. "Aw, I'm sorry."

"Sorry." Effie stuck out her chin. Her eyes were dark with the adults' perceived injustice. "But we weren't trying to hurt the old hats. We can't have any fun anymore. You don't let us play detectiving, Aunt Constance, and we can't play with Aunt Libby's hats." She swung out her arms. "What are we supposed to do for fun?"

Constance crossed her arms over her chest and shook her head. "I can barely keep up with you two and your fun times. Why don't you go across the street to Pierce's General Store and see if you can find some licorice sticks while Aunt Libby and I finish visiting?"

Effie's and Evan's eyes lit up. "All right! See you later!" They dashed out of the store, setting the brass bells above the door to ringing.

Libby always found it difficult to discipline her niece and nephew, as she thought of Effie and Evan, though they were truly her great-niece and great-nephew. She didn't feel old enough to be a great-aunt, but she couldn't deny her fifty-five years with Effie and Evan about. As if she needed more confirmation of her advancing age than her reflection in a mirror.

She looked down at Maria Louise in her wicker stroller. The little girl tipped her head back and looked up at the women with a wide-eyed, solemn gaze. The hat had been pushed down past her ears and covered her eyebrows.

Libby looked from the girl to Constance, struggling to keep from smiling. Constance's face showed a similar struggle. At the same moment, the women burst out laughing.

"I thought my corset stays would break from laughing so hard," Libby admitted minutes later, wiping tears of laughter from her face with a lace-edged handkerchief.

"Maria Louise and I had best get over to the general store and see what the Troublesome Twins are into now." Constance removed the bonnet from the little girl's head and handed it to Libby. Maria Louise immediately rubbed both her chubby little hands back and forth over her straight, short brown hair, sending the women into another spasm of laughter.

"We'll see you at dinner," Constance called over her shoulder minutes later, pushing the wicker carriage through the doorway.

Libby stared after them, smiling. *Life is so much richer since Constance and the twins moved here,* she thought. Only two years had passed since Constance married Justin Knight and moved to River's Edge with her brother's orphaned children. A year ago, Maria Louise had been born. Now the most important part of Libby's life centered around the Knight family.

She missed the husband she'd lost five years earlier, but she had a good life. She loved buying, designing, and selling hats. Church and the ladies sewing circle kept her busy socially. Ida Clayton, with whom she shared a home, provided companionship. And for the last two years, she'd been blessed with seeing Constance and the children every day. "Thank You for bringing them here, Lord," she whispered.

She bustled about the room, straightening a hat on a display stand, moving a ruffled, pink silk parasol to better advantage behind a group of ribboned bonnets, placing dainty white gloves with tiny pearl buttons beside a hat trimmed with lace, ribbon, and pearls. A few women stopped in. Some wanted only to spend a little of their afternoon admiring the new spring fashions. One planned to have the ostrich feathers replaced on her favorite bonnet. Another purchased a new spring hat. With her assistant, Miss Silvernail, out for the afternoon, Libby kept pleasantly busy with her customers.

When the rosewood clock on the wall chimed five o'clock, a cloud of regret slid across Libby's chest. She'd need to close the shop soon if she was to arrive at Constance's house in time for dinner. Constance hadn't mentioned that there would be other guests, but Libby was sure an eligible man would join them. All too often lately, such men turned up at Constance's dinners. Always Constance had a reasonable explanation, usually that the man had been doing business with Justin or that she was paying back a favor the man had done for the family. The men were all widowers. So far the guests had included the owner of a local sawmill, a bank officer, the owner of a sash firm, and a pinch-nosed schoolteacher.

Libby wasn't fooled. Constance was trying to find her a husband, or at least a beau. As if a woman of fifty-five needed a beau. Besides, she'd lived in River's Edge all her life. There wasn't a man in town she didn't know. If she wanted a beau or a husband, she'd make her own choice and set her cap for him. Perhaps it was time she came right out and told Constance so. Of course, she realized Constance only wanted her to find a husband because Constance was so happy married to Justin.

"She doesn't know there isn't room for another man in my heart," Libby whispered. "The two who are there fill it to the brim."

Libby's husband, Joshua Ward, had been a fine man. He hadn't been wealthy, but he'd held a respectable position as an accounting clerk in a local sawmill. He'd been well liked in the community. He'd shared Libby's love for the Lord. They hadn't had children, but their fellow church members and neighbors had been like family and still were for Libby. Libby and Joshua had respected and admired each other and shared a quiet, companionable life. Although Libby had loved him, he hadn't been her first love.

"If only Spencer had loved the Lord." The memory of him tightened her chest with longing.

She stopped before the wall mirror in an ornate walnut frame. Was there any resemblance between the reflection in that mirror and the young woman of twenty she'd been when she last saw Spencer?

Libby brushed a stray hair back over her ear. Her hand paused there, beside her face. The face in the mirror had deep wrinkles and faded blue eyes. Her hair was more gray than brown now. Her gaze traveled to her hand. Blood vessels showed blue through her skin. Libby sighed. "Barely a sign of the girl Spencer asked to marry him."

The spring breeze carried inside the scent of the earth awakening and the sound of birds returning to the northland. The last day she'd spent with Spencer had been just such a day. She moved to a window, from which the bluff where they'd picnicked that long-ago day could be seen above the town roofs.

The memory washed over her. . . .

❧

"I thought we'd never make it to the top!" Libby hugged her

waist. Her side was aching from the climb. Her legs were strong, but Spencer set quite a pace. He'd held her hand the entire way, helping her over the most difficult spots, yet the climb had seemed steep, particularly in the hooped gown, one of her most fashionable—and definitely her favorite. The tight corset didn't make it easy to breathe deeply, but she did like the way it cinched her waist.

She loved pretty clothes. They made her feel attractive. She knew she wasn't the best-looking young woman in town; in fact, she was plain. Her parents had told her so since she was little. "Better be pretty on the inside, Libby," her father would say, shaking his head, "because you sure ain't pretty on the outside." Her mother hadn't thought she was pretty on the inside, either. "You're never going to win a husband, Elizabeth Mann," her mother had flared many times through the years. "Plain of face and plain ornery by nature." Libby tried to be quiet and demure and giggly like other girls, but she couldn't seem to keep her lips sealed on her own opinions.

Spencer laughed and tugged at her hand. "Come along, lazybones. We're not quite to our spot yet. I want to sit at the bluff's edge, don't you?"

"Yes, the view's best there." She stopped, hugging her waist tighter with her free hand. "Let's rest a moment, please."

His arm slid about her waist, and she leaned into him, resting. "Are you all right, Libby?"

She scrunched her eyelids shut and forced a smile. "I've a stitch in my side, that's all. It will go away in a moment." They stood that way for a few minutes, Spencer waiting patiently while the pain subsided. She loved the way she felt cherished and sheltered, leaning against him.

When the pain was gone, they walked across the bluff. The light wind played with their hair and surrounded them with the happy smells of spring's renewing life. At the bluff's edge, they removed the blanket from the basket Spencer had been carrying and spread it out. The picnic lunch was simple: biscuits and ham and dried-apple pie. It didn't matter. The only thing that mattered was that the two of them were together. They had so little time. He'd been away most of the winter, working as a lumberjack in the northern forest. Now that the river was free of ice, he was back in River's Edge and would be working at a local sawmill, eleven hours a day, six days a week. The only time they would have together would be Sundays, like today.

The view from the bluff was spectacular. Beneath them, the wide, blue Mississippi River flowed past. Across the river, the view mirrored the side of the river where they sat: trees, with pale green buds hinting at the splendor of their coming summer dress, climbed three-fourths of the way up the steep sides; from there to the top was a wonderful expanse of limestone, pale yellow in the sunshine. On top of the bluff, trees again reached to the sky. In the valley to the right of where they sat, River's Edge stood bravely on the riverbank.

A long, white, elegant steamboat, its tall black smokestacks trailing streams of gray smoke, made its way northward.

"Someday, I'm going to work on one of them." Spencer circled his knees with his arms. "I'm going to travel the river, see the big cities to the south. No more spending my winters in lumber camps."

Libby's chest clenched. She plucked at a new blade of grass, keeping her gaze on it. "If you work on a steamboat, we'll be apart as surely as when you are at the lumber camp."

She could tell from the corner of her eye that he turned from the river to look at her. "Ah, Libby, don't you know I'd take you along to see the world with me?"

Her gaze darted to his. His voice had been thick with emotion. His eyes were dark with it. He slid a hand behind her neck, then slowly bridged the short distance between them. His lips were gentle, his kiss lingering. With a slight sigh, she responded, leaning against him. His kiss shut out the world. Nothing existed for her but Spencer.

Minutes later, he pulled back, laughing shakily. She understood that self-conscious laugh. Their kisses were too sweet, too intimate, too dangerous. Better to stop.

He laid down on his back, resting his head in her lap. Her

huge skirt billowed out around him. "Brought something back from the camp for you."

"Whatever could you have found for me in a lumber camp?"

"Didn't exactly find it. I made it." He reached for his jacket, which he'd taken off when they sat down, and plunged a hand into one pocket. "Close your eyes and hold out your hand."

She did as he asked. A moment later, she felt something hard with a smooth finish in her palm. She opened her eyes. It was a bird carved from wood. "It's beautiful!" She stroked the goose's delicately carved wings and long, graceful neck. Lifting the bird to her face, she breathed deeply. "I can smell the forests where you worked."

"They were beautiful in winter, with snow covering the pines. And the silence! Like a church. I wish I could have shared the beauty of it with you."

They smiled into each other's eyes. Libby was filled with sweet wonder that he should want to share something as simple as a winter scene with her.

Spencer lifted his eyebrows. "Of course, everything about the forest wasn't beautiful. It was mighty cold! And those bearded, swearing lumbermen didn't make the forest any prettier. Nothing like a few days with them to make a man miss a woman."

Libby laughed with him, pleased and a little embarrassed at his implication. She changed the subject back to his gift. "I didn't know you could carve."

"I didn't either. Believe me, this wasn't my first attempt. I whittled a number of them before I made a couple that satisfied me." He pulled something out of his other pocket and held it out. "I wanted one for both of us. I've been told geese mate for life." His voice had dropped. "Once a goose and a gander take a liking to each other, they never part. That's what I want for us: to be together forever."

"I want that, too." Her throat was so tight it hurt to speak the words. He'd told her before that he loved her, but he'd never spoken of their future. She looked down at his dear, wide face, the straight, blond hair that glistened in the spring sunshine, looked into the blue eyes that were watching her. Love filled her chest until there was no more room for it, and it overflowed. She could feel her smile trembling.

"I hated being away from you this winter, Libby."

"Naturally, since you were in the middle of a forest with nothing but trees, men, and snow to keep you company."

He drew her hands down until her arms circled his head. He held his goose beak-to-beak with the one in her hands, moving it slightly back and forth in a teasing, flirtatious motion. "Won't you tell me you missed me a *little* bit?"

His low, intimate tone sent shivers through her. She could feel his breath against her hands. She tried to keep a teasing tone in her own voice. "I missed you a big bit, Spencer."

"I knew it!" His free hand clasped one of hers. He grinned up at her, triumph sparkling in his eyes.

"You are abominable!" She tugged at her hand, and he released it, laughing.

"Tell me how you missed me."

She shook her head, her long, fashionable, pale brown curls swinging against her cheeks. "I will not."

"Then I'll tell you what it was like missing you." He curled his fingers around hers, cradling her hand against his chest. He closed his eyes. "Lying in my bunk at night, I'd see your face. I'd go over it in every detail, remembering the softness and sweet smell of your hair, those blue eyes that blaze when you're upset with me, your cute, pointed chin, and the line of your throat above your high-collared gowns." He smiled, as if he enjoyed the memories. "Mostly, I remembered your smile and how soft your lips were when I kissed you good-bye when I left for the lumber camp." He touched his lips to her fingers. "Did you do that, Libby?" he asked in a whisper. "Did you think about me that way while I was gone?"

Heat spread up Libby's throat and over her cheeks. "Yes."

"Good." His smile widened.

"You're impossible." She tried unsuccessfully to draw her hand back.

"It's only the two of us here. You don't have to act like

there's a prim and proper chaperon listening. We can speak the truth to each other without embarrassment. Isn't that the way it should be?"

"I–I don't know."

His eyelids flew open. "You don't think we should tell each other the truth?"

"Quit mocking me. Of course I think we should speak the truth, but proper manners require certain things be left unsaid until—" She pressed her lips together firmly. She'd already said too much, as usual.

"Until what? Until people are married to each other?"

Libby kept her gaze trained on the wooden geese on Spencer's chest. "Well, yes."

"How do people know they want to marry each other if they don't tell each other what they feel before they're man and wife?"

She didn't have an answer when he put it in those terms. She felt his gaze burning into her. Finally, she could ignore it no longer and reluctantly turned to meet it.

His gaze claimed hers. "Will you marry me, Libby?"

two

Libby's heart smashed against her ribs. Her hands froze on the wooden goose. *Did he really ask me to marry him, or did I imagine it?* she wondered. She couldn't tear her gaze from Spencer's.

"Libby?" His blond brows slipped together. Uncertainty clouded his eyes. "I love you, Libby."

"I love you, too," she whispered.

Her answer routed the doubt from his eyes. "Is that a yes to my proposal?"

"I want to marry you, Spencer, and spend the rest of my life with you."

A grin filled his face. He sat up so quickly the wooden geese that had rested on his chest tumbled to the ground. "Come here, my future wife."

She allowed him to draw her into his embrace, returning his kiss, but his arms weren't the same as they'd been earlier. The world didn't disappear. Instead, worry over the way Spencer would react to the rest of her answer made the embrace bittersweet.

After a few minutes, he pulled back far enough to look into her eyes and smile. "Mrs. Spencer Matthews. Has a nice sound to it, don't you think?"

"The nicest." Her throat hurt so much that she could barely get the words out.

"Let's get married this summer. I don't want to wait a day longer than necessary to begin our life together."

Her laugh sounded more like a sob to her. His eagerness touched her. How blessed, to be loved this way! "Don't you think that's a little soon?"

"Why? We love each other." He raised his eyebrows. "Your parents won't object to me, will they?"

"I hardly think so." Her parents were surprised any men were interested in her. That Spencer wanted to marry her would surprise them but surely not offend them.

"I suppose you're worried it will take awhile to plan the wedding."

"No." She took as deep a breath as her corset allowed. "Spencer, you know how important my faith in Jesus is," she began.

He nodded. "Sure. You don't think I'll ask you to give it up? I might not share your faith, but I have to admit, it's one of the things I like and admire about you."

She took both his hands in hers. "I love you, Spencer, but I can't marry you until you believe in Jesus, too, and He is the most important part of your life."

He stared at her. He looked as stunned as though the earth had stopped spinning. "You can't mean that."

Libby bit her lips and nodded.

Spencer yanked his hands from hers. "I may not believe in your God, but that doesn't make me too dirty to marry, does it?" He was yelling now. "Faith in God isn't something a man can whip up just because a woman wants him to!"

Libby winced. "I know."

"What makes you so much better than I am, just because you believe what somebody wrote a couple thousand years ago?"

"I don't believe I'm better than you, Spencer."

He hadn't waited for her reply. He was still yelling, bouncing his fingertips off his chest. "What about me is so awful that you can't abide the thought of marrying me?"

"Nothing." Misery ribboned through her at the hurt her words had caused him, at her inability to take the words back and heal the wound.

"Didn't I stop smoking and drinking for you?"

She nodded.

"What more can I do to prove how much I love you, to prove I'm a good man? What does it matter what I believe about God if my actions are good?" He didn't wait for her to answer. He went on with similar arguments until he appeared to run out of words.

It was then Libby tried to explain. "It's my faith that makes me who I am, Spencer. My values are determined by my faith. My strength in hard times is supplied by my faith. My faith is a beacon light when I don't know which way to turn. It's my guide. How can two people travel through life together if they don't have the same guide?"

"Travel with that invisible guide, if that's your choice. God won't give you a home or a family like I would. His arms won't be around you when life hurts and you need a shoulder to cry on. He won't be there beside you, telling you He loves you every day, like I would. You think He's more important than a man who loves you—you just spend your life with Him, Libby Mann!"

"I'm not saying I won't marry you, Spencer. I'm only asking you to wait, until. . ."

"Until I believe in your God? In a God you believe doesn't want you to marry a man you love, a man who loves you? What kind of God is that to believe in? If you won't marry me unless I believe in an ornery God like that, you won't ever marry me, because I don't want your God in my life." Spencer turned on his heel and marched toward the path that led down from the bluff.

"Spencer, come back!" Tears heated Libby's eyes, but she could still see he wasn't returning. She sank to her knees, heedless of the grass and dirt. Her chest felt like it was in a vise. "I didn't mean to hurt him, Lord," she whispered between sobs. "Please, bring him back!"

She'd always known, of course, that she shouldn't have allowed Spencer to court her when he didn't share her faith, but she'd been so attracted to him, right from the beginning! At her request, he'd given up the awful-smelling cigars and the liquor with barely more than a murmur of protest. "I always believed he would eventually believe in You, Lord. I still do."

Yet that belief didn't stop the pain. She tried to push away the fear that Spencer might never return, but the fear only grew, filling her stomach and heart and mind.

꼭

Libby turned from the window and walked slowly across the shop, stopping in front of the walnut-framed mirror. Spencer hadn't returned. Not that day, not ever.

Three days later, when she'd heard the rumor about Spencer that was flying around town, she hadn't believed it. Two days after that, walking down the short, dirt main street, she'd met Spencer with a young woman clinging to his arm. Color had darkened his face when Libby's gaze met his. Then his gaze had darted away, but not before she saw the shame in his blue eyes. That was when she knew the rumor was true. That was when her world changed forever. That was when her heart was torn open to never fully heal.

After leaving her on the bluff, Spencer had come back to River's Edge and gone on a drinking spree. While drunk, he'd eloped. Before long, he and his new wife left town.

At first, Libby had thought she would surely die. After months passed and it seemed her heart hadn't begun to heal, she had to cling hard to the Lord's promises in Psalm 40 to keep from wishing she *could* die. "I waited patiently for the Lord; and he inclined unto me, and heard my cry. He brought me up also out of an horrible pit, out of the miry clay, and set my foot upon a rock, and established my goings."

The pain in her heart had made it seem the Lord hadn't heard her cry. When the pain seemed unendurable and she was crying out to the Lord asking how Spencer could have married someone else and taken away all chance they would spend their life together, she would repeat the verse, reminding herself that eventually God would lift her out of that terrible place and life would be good again.

After a year had passed, she began to see a glimmer of that good place. At first, there were only a couple hours a day she could make it through without crying. When the time came that she could make it through an entire day—not every day, but some days—without crying, she knew she would live to see the promise fulfilled. And she knew that even when she hadn't been able to see the light, God had been healing her heart.

She'd learned she could live through anything, leaning on Christ, who had promised never to leave her or forsake her. From that point on, she gave up the right to mollycoddle herself.

Even in the midst of her pain, she knew that how Spencer left didn't matter. Unless he had chosen to believe in Christ and follow His teachings, she and Spencer couldn't have had a life together anyway.

She prayed for him every time she thought of him. Had her prayers been answered yet? Had he ever come to believe?

She wondered, as she so often had, whether he was still alive. His family had left River's Edge soon after he and his wife had moved. Was his wife still alive? Where were they living? Did they have children?

"Thirty-five years!" she whispered. How could her heart still yearn for him? If she'd married him, their marriage wouldn't have been anything like the one she and Joshua had shared. That love had been good and strong but different from the love she'd shared with Spencer.

She studied her reflection. *It's not the face of the young girl Spencer proposed to,* she thought again. Her hair wasn't worn in the fashion of 1860, with dangling curls beside her ears. Now a curly fringe of bangs topped her wrinkled face, and the rest of the graying hair was caught back in a high bun.

"Well, what can a woman expect after fifty-five years of living? The body is meant to get older. Doesn't the Good Book tell us that gray hair is a sign of wisdom?"

I don't feel wise, she thought. *Wiser about a host of things than when I was twenty, but not wise. Sometimes I think there's more things I don't have answers to today than back then.*

Spencer's face flashed into her mind, that dear face that would always be twenty-three years old to her. "One thing I know; I would give him the same answer today." She saw the pain and fury fill his eyes and face as they had that day, felt his pain and fury scorch her heart once more. She had wanted so deeply to marry him. "How could I say yes, Lord, when he didn't share my love for You? What kind of life could we have had together when we didn't share a trust in You?"

She sighed and turned her back on the mirror. If she didn't hurry, she'd be late for Constance's dinner. She felt as though she were dragging her heart along behind her when she carried the hat the children had been playing with into the back room, where Miss Silvernail would change the ribbons the next day.

She'd barely entered the room when the bells above the front door jangled. Impatience shot through her. After wallowing in sad memories, she was in no mood to wait on a last-minute customer. Habit formed from years of running her own shop came to her aid. She took a deep breath, straightened her shoulders, and went back into the shop.

A man her own age or older, wearing a jacket trimmed in gold braid, stood just inside the door, glancing about the room with the bewildered expression she saw on most men's faces when they entered her hat shop. His skin was weathered and wrinkled, his thick hair and bushy eyebrows were white with a tinge of dark gray. A trim, gray-and-white beard framed his wide face.

She smiled and forced friendliness into her voice. "May I help you, sir?"

The man jerked about, staring at her without answering.

She laced her fingers together in front of her and tried again. "Is there something I can help you find?"

The thick eyebrows met. His gaze searched her face until she wanted to wiggle in discomfort. "Libby?"

Her heart dropped to her toes. She'd recognize that voice anywhere. "Spencer!"

three

Libby had dreamed of this meeting for over half her life, and now that Spencer was here, she couldn't think of a word to say. All she could do was stare at him, drink in the wonder of his presence, experience the joy flooding her.

Reality tempered her joy. *He wouldn't be in a women's hat shop if he weren't looking for a bonnet or accessories for a woman in his life,* she reminded herself. *At least I know he's still alive. Thank You, Lord!*

Spencer dropped his own black, braid-trimmed hat on a table amidst an assortment of dainty spring bonnets and started toward her, holding out both hands. "Libby! How good to see you again." His deep voice rumbled across the room. Delight filled his creased and tanned face.

His height and broad shoulders dwarfed everything in the room, though Libby admitted to herself that even if that weren't the case, he was the only thing she would see.

She allowed him to take her hands. They were swallowed up in his. She was vaguely aware that his hands were calloused. With a start, she realized that, with the exception of Constance's husband, no man had touched her ungloved hands since her own husband had died, five years ago.

It wasn't only his voice that hadn't changed. His smile was the same, as were his blue eyes. To Libby's dismay, she found they had the same effect on her they'd had when she was twenty.

He squeezed her hands and grinned down at her. "How are you, Libby?"

"Fine. I'm fine." That sounded inane, even to her own ears.

"You look grand."

She tugged at her hands, recalling all too vividly the view in the mirror only minutes earlier. He released her hands immediately. *He's older, too,* she reminded herself silently, trying desperately to reassure herself. *We've both aged, and we look it. Nothing to be ashamed of in that. Silly to worry what he thinks of my looks, anyway. He's married to someone else.* Still, she did worry. A hand went to the lock of hair at her temple that was always falling out of place.

"Um, your boat must have landed in town." She pressed her lips together to keep back a groan. Another silly comment.

"Not exactly." He stuffed his hands into his trouser pockets and leaned back against a display table, looking entirely at ease. "The boat I came upriver on docked here. I'm retired." His eyes widened. "You knew I was a steamboat captain!"

Embarrassment warmed her cheeks. "I. . .someone mentioned it years ago." The twinkle in his eyes increased her embarrassment. She turned to the counter behind her and unnecessarily readjusted a French bonnet on its cast-iron stand. "Did you wish to purchase a gift? For your wife, perhaps?"

"No, Libby."

She heard his footsteps cross the wooden floor and stop behind her. Her heartbeat quickened at his nearness. In an attempt to slow it, she closed her eyes and took a deep breath.

"I didn't come to purchase a gift." The intensity in his voice sent shivers down her spine. "I came to see you."

Libby's eyelids snapped open. Her heart raced out of control, rejoicing in the knowledge that he'd wanted to see her. Her mind screamed that his coming was wrong, as was her joy in seeing him.

"My wife died three years ago."

Relief that he wasn't being unfaithful left Libby suddenly weak. She held on to the counter's edge for a moment to steady herself. "I'm sorry." Taking a deep breath, she turned to face him. "I truly am sorry."

"Margaret was a good wife to me. I did my best to be a good husband to her."

"I'm sure you did. I would expect nothing less." Libby tried to ignore the pain in her chest, ashamed to be jealous of the woman who had shared his life and had left it so soon.

The blue eyes she remembered so well studied hers. "Even though I was a faithful husband, we both know why I married her."

Libby stared at her hands. They were clasped together so tightly the knuckles were white.

"I stopped to see an old friend today. He told me that your husband is dead, too."

"He died five years ago."

"I'm sorry." Spencer cleared his throat. "I wouldn't have come here today if he was still alive. You know that, don't you?"

Libby nodded, still staring at her hands. Of course, she believed him. He'd never before looked her up when his boat stopped at River's Edge.

He rested a hand over her clasped ones. She caught her breath sharply, marveling at the gentleness in his touch.

"Will you have dinner with me? I want to hear all about your life, everything you've done in the years since I left River's Edge."

In the years since you left us, she silently amended his words. "I have another obligation."

"Tomorrow evening, then?"

She smiled, aware her lips were trembling. "That would be nice."

"Shall I pick you up here, about this time?"

"Yes, that will be fine."

His hand still covered hers. He seemed reluctant to leave, and she was certainly reluctant to see him go.

Slowly, he slipped his hand away. "I'd best be going or I'll make you late for your engagement." He took a couple steps backward. "Until tomorrow."

"Yes, until tomorrow." Tomorrow! What promise that wonderful word held!

He picked up his gold-trimmed hat from the table where he'd dropped it. In the open doorway, he stopped, staring across the room at her, smiling. Then, raising a large palm held up in a silent good-bye, he left.

Libby collapsed back against the counter. He'd returned! "Why has he sought me out after all this time, Lord?" Her thoughts spun. So many questions, but three stood out boldly from the rest: Was he planning to live in River's Edge? Would he want to court her again? Most important, had he come to a faith in Christ?

The clock on the wall struck six-thirty.

"Oh, my!" Libby hurried into the back room and slung her elbow-length cape over her shoulders. Stopping in front of the wall mirror in the shop, she pinned her hat on with shaking fingers.

She almost dropped the key when locking the front door. *How will I ever keep my mind on conversation at dinner tonight?* she wondered, her heels clipping on the boardwalk. *It will be easier if I'm mistaken about Constance's intentions in inviting me and it's only her family this evening.*

❧

Tomorrow! Tomorrow! Tomorrow! The word rang through Captain Spencer Matthews's mind like a church bell pealing news of hope and cheer. *This time tomorrow, we'll be together.* He'd daydreamed about that time for so many years that he could barely believe it was almost here.

He moved along the boardwalk, smiling and nodding to complete strangers, wanting to shout his good news. He chuckled. Best wait for that until he'd received what he came to River's Edge for—Libby's hand in marriage.

What if she says no? The words crept into his mind. He tried to push them aside. He wouldn't accept the possibility she would refuse him.

Of course, there's that faith stuff she holds so dear to get past. Another thought he tried to push aside. Over the years, he'd come to believe he'd been a fool to allow her faith to keep them apart. Surely she would have realized, too, that she'd been wrong to think such a thing should separate them. *We're both too old and wise to let silly superstitions push away love.*

The early evening skies were bright as day. Usually he was

glad for springtime's longer days. Today he was eager for night to come. The sooner it came, the sooner tomorrow would arrive. Of course, there'd be all those hours to live through tomorrow until he could call for Libby, but—he shrugged, chuckling at himself.

The sight of his hotel brought sour memories. He'd awakened in a hotel the morning—or rather, afternoon—following his marriage to Margaret. His head had been pounding and his eyesight blurred, but he'd recognized the woman in his room and had enough sense to demand what she was doing there.

The feeling of desolation he'd experienced when Margaret said she was his wife washed over him again now. At first, he'd insisted she was lying. He'd stopped that when she showed him the marriage certificate. Hopelessness such as he'd never known before or since had swallowed him up whole. In one foolish move, he'd changed the entire course of his life. He'd cut himself off forever from Libby.

Or at least so he'd thought until today.

His steps quickened. Life had given him a second chance. *This time, I won't throw away our future,* he thought. *This time, I won't stop asking Libby to marry me until she says yes.*

four

As Libby had feared, another single man had been invited to dinner: Pastor Daniel Green, who had moved to town a few weeks earlier. He must have arrived at the Knights' only moments before her, as he was still in the wide, walnut-paneled entry hall when she arrived.

It could have been worse, she admitted silently. They'd met at church, of course, and she knew him to be a pleasant, easy-going man. Certainly there wasn't a better-looking man her age in River's Edge. *Except Spencer.* The pastor was a slender man. His dark hair had less gray and his face fewer lines than most men his age.

Libby unpinned her hat, removed it and her cape, and handed them to Constance, wishing she could simply leave and go home. She tried to overcome her frustration and resistance. It wouldn't do to spoil Constance's dinner party by acting standoffish.

"It must be difficult, moving to a town where you don't know anyone." *He probably has a month's worth of invitations already, from people like Constance, who are eager to introduce him to their unmarried friends. He must find the presence of an unexpected and marriageable dinner guest as unpleasant as I. I've only Constance trying to marry me off. He'll have most of the matrons in River's Edge trying to find him the proper mate.* The realization tempered her distaste of the situation and made her more tolerant.

"It's easier for a pastor than for most people, I think," he answered, "though it was easier to move into new communities when my wife was alive. The church members always draw a pastor into the community quickly."

Constance turned from the hall closet and slipped an arm through Libby's. Starting for the parlor, she explained to Pastor

26

Green, "I married Justin and moved here from Chicago two years ago with my eight-year-old niece and nephew after my brother and his wife died. Aunt Libby took us under her wing. We're the only family either of us has left. I'd like her to move in with us, but she insists on living in her own home with her friend, Mrs. Clayton." Constance gave an exaggerated sigh. "So we must settle for Aunt Libby's presence at dinners whenever she can work us into her schedule."

Her words further eased Libby's tension; perhaps the pastor wouldn't think her a manhunting female after all.

Racing steps caught the adults' attention. Constance shook her head. "I apologize for the children. I admonish them numerous times daily to walk, not run, in the house, but the admonitions fall on deaf ears."

Libby smiled. "I believe the children, Effie especially, are simply so excited with life that they can't bear to move through it at a pace as slow as a walk. A wonderful way to approach life, don't you think?"

"I do, indeed."

Libby liked the way the pastor greeted the children warmly and included them in his conversation while they visited with the Knights in the parlor.

It was only a few minutes before the maid announced dinner and they moved into the formal dining room. The chandelier sparkled above the elegantly appointed rosewood table. Cream-colored velvet draperies and satin-striped wallpaper lent a tranquil atmosphere.

As owner and president of the local bank, Justin Knight was adept in social graces, for which Libby was never more grateful. Instead of trying to carry on a conversation with the pastor, she allowed Justin and Constance to do so.

While they talked, her mind drifted back to the unexpected meeting with Spencer. Her heart quickened at the thought of him. His smiling eyes filled her memory. Watching Pastor Green, she couldn't help but compare him to Spencer. They were nothing alike physically. She was sure they were nothing alike in personality, either.

They were barely into the main course when Effie piped up. "Did you hear about the ghost?"

The word "ghost" effectively brought a halt to the adult conversation. Everyone turned to stare at her. Effie's grin spread across her wide, freckled face. Libby slipped her napkin over her mouth to hide her smile at Effie's evident self-satisfaction.

Justin set down his fork and frowned. "What's this about a ghost?"

Effie leaned forward. Her brown eyes danced with excitement. "Evan and me heard about it at Pierce's General Store this afternoon."

Evan's head bobbed emphatically. "A bunch of people were talking about it."

Effie's voice dropped an octave and trembled. "There were strange, moving lights on the bluffs north of town last night." She lifted her fingers just above the edge of the table and wiggled them.

A shiver ran down Libby's spine. *Stop it!* she admonished herself. *You don't even believe in ghosts!*

"Don't be silly." Justin's voice sounded hoarse. "Pastor Green can tell you there are no such things as ghosts. Even if there were, lights on the bluff are no sign of ghosts."

"He's right," Constance agreed. "Why would ghosts need lights? If there were lights on the bluff, it's because there were people on the bluff."

"But they were on the *side* of the bluff," Effie explained, not willing to let go of her ghost theory so easily.

"That's right." Evan jumped in, his voice eager, his brown eyes huge. "People might walk on top of the bluff, but they wouldn't walk on the sides of the bluff, at night, would they?"

He's right, Libby thought. To try to climb the bluff's steep walls at night or walk the few crumbling paths along them in the dark would be a fool's mission. She was sure similar thoughts were flashing through Justin's mind, as he hesitated before answering Effie.

"Maybe it was just a traveler, staying overnight in one of the caves."

"Why wouldn't he stay in a hotel?" Effie asked.

"Maybe he didn't have enough money," Justin answered, a bit lamely.

Effie picked up her fork and went back to her dinner. "I think it was ghosts."

"Me, too." Evan dug into his meal, imitating his sister as usual.

Libby wondered uneasily what Pastor Green thought of the children's talk of ghosts. He hadn't said a word, and if he disapproved, his face didn't reveal the fact.

Justin changed the subject, speaking of a newspaper article that reported a continuing upswing in the nation's economy. Pastor Green followed Justin's lead, and soon the adults had forgotten the subject of ghosts and were discussing the wonderful recovery the country was making from the financial depression that had started two years ago.

"I'm not educated in things of the financial world like you, Mr. Knight," the pastor said. "Still, I enjoy reading the articles arguing the benefits of a silver standard as opposed to a gold standard."

"That's what the ghost is looking for." Effie didn't bother looking for the adults' reaction this time. She just took another bite of roast beef.

Justin carefully set down his fork. Libby expected he was counting to ten. "*What* is he looking for?" His voice was tight with exasperation.

Effie looked up, raising her eyebrows beneath her thick bangs. She swallowed her bite. "Gold, of course."

"Oh, Effie, really." Constance shook her head.

"It's true." Evan straightened up in his chair. "That's what the people at the store said."

Justin closed his eyes and opened them again. "What would a ghost need with gold?"

"The gold belongs to him," Evan informed him.

"How can gold belong to a ghost?" His frustrated voice, even more than his words, revealed his belief that all this talk was foolishness.

Even if Justin's faith didn't encourage him to not believe in ghosts, Libby thought, *his practical banker nature wouldn't let him believe in them!*

Effie spread her hands palm up on each side of her plate. She looked at Justin as though she couldn't believe he could be so simple. "It belonged to him before he became a ghost, of course."

"That's right," Evan supported his sister again. "He hid it in a cave in the bluffs before he died."

"*Who* hid it before he died?" The question slipped out before Libby thought.

"The captain of that old steamboat that ran up on the sandbar below the bluffs last month," Effie answered.

Evan nodded.

"Where did you children come up with such an implausible story?" Constance asked.

Effie frowned. "What's im–implaws. . ."

"Implausible," Constance finished. "It means not believable."

"We told you," Evan reminded her. "At the general store."

"When the boat got stuck," Effie explained, "the captain was afraid people would steal the gold, so he hid it. After he hid it and came back to the boat, he got sick. The men who worked for him tried to help him, but they couldn't, and he died."

Evan broke in. "But before he died, he whispered something. The men couldn't understand all of it—"

"But they heard the words *gold* and *bluff.*" Effie's voice was thick and low and trembly.

Libby shivered, even while scolding herself for reacting so strongly to Effie's storytelling skills. She remembered Captain Hollingsworth's death the month before. His heart, the doctor had said. The steamboat was still sitting on the sandbar. It had been one of the first steamboats on the upper Mississippi this year, arriving almost during rather than after the spring thaw.

Constance rose. "I believe we've had more than enough of this ghost business for one evening. I want you two to go upstairs and get dressed for bed."

Evan's mouth dropped. "But we haven't had dessert yet!"

Effie crossed her arms and leaned back in her chair, glaring. "It isn't fair! We were just telling you what people said."

"Mrs. Kelly can bring your dessert to your rooms." Controlled Constance was firm, unflustered, as usual. "Justin and I will be up to hear your prayers later."

"But—" Effie started.

"Now," Justin ordered. "And no 'detectiving.' "

Libby hid another smile. Detectiving, or eavesdropping, on the Knights' guests was the children's favorite pastime.

I wonder if Spencer would like Effie and Evan? Libby thought. When they were young, she'd enjoyed watching Spencer with his siblings and neighborhood children. He'd never shooed them away but played and teased and laughed with them whenever they came around. *But he's almost an old man now. Maybe he doesn't care for children any longer.*

After warm hugs and good nights all around, the children headed off to bed.

"I do hope you don't think we raised the children to believe in ghosts, Pastor." Constance looked apologetic.

He gave her an easy smile. "I didn't hear anything that sounded as though you or your husband were encouraging their belief. Besides, the children heard the story from adult townspeople. It isn't easy to teach children to know when to believe other adults."

Libby was pleased with his reply.

The conversation moved on. Libby put on a polite smile and let her mind drift to Spencer. Though Pastor Green was a pleasant man, she wasn't in the least interested in knowing him better. How could any man compete with the excitement of seeing Spencer again?

Libby was glad when Justin offered her a ride home. She had been wondering how she would turn down the pastor's offer to walk her home, if he should make such an offer, as Constance's bachelor dinner guests normally did.

Libby breathed a huge sigh of relief when she closed her

front door. The dinner was behind her, and her own home was dark and quiet. Ida, her housemate, had retired for the night.

Upstairs, Libby slipped into her long, white, cotton night-gown and climbed into bed, pulling the wedding-ring quilt, which had been a wedding gift from her church's sewing circle, up under her chin. Finally, she was alone and could let her thoughts drift uninterrupted to Spencer.

She found herself having one conversation after another with him in her mind, asking him all the things she'd wanted to ask through the years and hearing him declare his undying love for her.

"Stop it!" She sat up suddenly and pressed her hands over her ears to shut out the words that seemed as loud inside her head as if they'd actually been spoken. "I mustn't think these things. He only invited me to have dinner because I'm an old friend." At least, that was all she dared let herself think. If she allowed herself to hope it was something more and it wasn't, there would be so much pain to endure!

"Besides," she whispered into the night, "we don't know each other anymore. We may find we don't even like each other now."

In her heart, she didn't believe that was possible. She didn't dare dwell on her greatest question: Had Spencer ever come to believe in the God she loved so well?

five

Libby stuck a pearl-tipped hat pin into the dainty spring bonnet atop her head and studied her reflected image with anxious eyes. The fashionable hat was darling. She'd seen one just like it in the latest issue of *The Ladies' Standard.*

She dragged a bentwood chair from the workroom. Climbing onto it, she tried to view her full form. The image in the mirror was of the beautiful brown moire satin gown—at least, the portion from just below her bust to just above her knees. "Why didn't I think to ask Spencer to meet me at my home, where I have a full-length mirror? Maybe I should go next door and use the dress shop's mirror."

She shook her head resolutely. Her housemate, Mrs. Ida Clayton, owned that shop. When she'd told Ida she had a dinner engagement, Ida had assumed it was with the Knights. Libby hadn't corrected her. She wasn't ready to discuss Spencer's reappearance.

Libby gave her attention back to her gown. The mirror reflected her small waist, accentuated by the brown satin bow, and narrow lace wrists topped with tiny brown bows at the bottom of leg-o'-mutton sleeves. She bent at the waist to view the top of the gown. Smiled in satisfaction. Creamy-white Venetian lace rippled over her shoulders and circled her neck.

Is it too fancy? she wondered. She didn't want Spencer to think the night was *too* important to her, but she simply couldn't bring herself to wear one of her working dresses to dinner. She'd brought the dress along to the shop this morning, after perusing all the gowns and shirtwaists and skirts in her closet. The last hour the shop had been open she'd been hopelessly inattentive to her clients, fearful she wouldn't have time to change before Spencer arrived.

She took a deep breath. "Still covering yourself with beautiful gowns, the same as when you were young, hoping their beauty will make up for your plain features, aren't you? You'd think after fifty-five years of living, you'd have learned you are an ugly duckling and won't ever become a beautiful swan."

Ducklings never grow into swans, a voice in her head seemed to say, *but they become beautiful ducks, and that is what they are born to become.*

Libby shook her head. The wrinkled, skinny face in the mirror wasn't beautiful, no matter what fairy stories and silly voices in her head said.

The brass bells tinkled merrily. Libby swung to face the door, grabbing the chair's back to keep her balance. "Spencer!"

"Evening, Libby." He crossed the room in a few large steps. "May I help you down?"

He acted as though it was perfectly normal for a woman to be standing on a chair hunched over a mirror. Though his hand was a strong support, she felt clumsy climbing down from the chair. It was mortifying, him coming in on her that way, when she'd spent so much time hoping to make a good impression on him. Her cheeks stung with embarrassment.

He didn't appear to notice. Still holding her hand, he swept her with his gaze. "You look lovely, Libby."

Her embarrassment turned to pleasure. He'd always had that rare quality in a man of noticing a woman's attire. "Thank you." This time, her tone was warm. "You look quite the gentleman yourself."

His chuckle shook his broad chest and brought a twinkle to his eyes. He fingered the silk ascot at his neck. "You needn't look so shocked. Steamboat captains have plenty of gentlemen passengers to show us how we're expected to dress as landlubbers."

Flustered, she didn't attempt a reply. She knew, of course, that captains were the steamboats' hosts. He must have entertained many wealthy, prominent people in his time. Did he think her hopelessly unsophisticated and inexperienced in travel? "I'll get my cape and gloves."

When she turned from locking the shop's front door, he reached for her hand, and drew it through his arm. Her heart pounded madly, walking with him down the boardwalk toward the tall brick hotel where they would dine. Though she could tell he was shortening his steps for her, she took two steps to his one. She didn't mind; she was normally quick paced.

Self-consciously, she returned smiles and greetings from surprised townspeople they met on the way. It felt good to walk with Spencer so intimately. Good, but scary.

Is it safe, spending an evening with him? It was a question she'd been avoiding for twenty-four hours. Would the evening ahead open all the torn places in her heart that had taken so many years to heal?

The small town was fortunate to have a lovely dining room that catered to the traveling public brought by the steamboats in the past and railroads today. The room looked especially attractive to her this evening. Fine walnut chairs upholstered in maroon velvet and linen-covered tables filled the room beneath a crystal chandelier. Fine art in ornate frames decorated the walls, covered in stripes of pearl and rose.

The waitress smiled at her knowingly after leading them to their table. Libby resented her look, yet was glad she seated them far enough from other guests for private conversation.

When Spencer had ordered steak dinners for them, the time came to face each other and actually talk. Libby's gloved fingers played nervously with the linen napkin in her lap. There were so many things she wanted to ask him, she didn't know where to start! She needn't have worried. Spencer had questions of her.

"Do your children live in River's Edge, Libby?"

"I have no children."

Sympathy darkened his blue eyes. "I'm sorry. I can't imagine you without children. You always loved them so."

"When Joshua and I met, I was working as an assistant in a small millinery department in a local store. Joshua knew I enjoyed the work. He agreed I might continue it until we began a family." She looked down at her lap. "The children never came."

"I'm sorry." His voice was a hoarse whisper.

Was he remembering the times they'd spent with his younger siblings when they were little more than children themselves? Libby put on a smile and lifted her face. "Did you and your wife have children?"

"Two boys. Fine, strapping lads. Henry and Alexander. They're grown now, with families of their own."

"You're a grandfather?"

He nodded, grinning. "Two boys and a girl so far."

Delight for him filled her. "How wonderful for you! I can picture you bouncing a baby on your knee."

"The children have me wrapped around their little fingers, I shamelessly admit."

She smiled. "I've a nephew and two nieces in town who have me in the same position. A rather nice place to be, isn't it?"

"That it is. I'm glad you have children in your life."

"I am, too. God has been good to me. My niece, Constance, moved to River's Edge two years ago and married the banker, Justin Knight." She told him about Effie and Evan and the baby, Maria Louise. Tales of Effie and Evan's attempts at "detectiving" filled the time with shared laughter until the steaks were served.

"Where do your boys live?"

"In St. Louis, queen of the steamboat cities." His smile faded. "Margaret and I moved there when we left here."

Libby looked down at her plate. "That makes sense. You always loved the river. You must have enjoyed being a steamboat captain."

"That I did. I didn't start out as a captain, of course. Must have held down most every position there is on a boat, including that of the lowly cabin boy. I kept my dream in mind, and eventually, I owned my own boat. During the War Between the States, it was a boom time for steamboaters. Troops and supplies were shipped by steamboat, so many were built to handle the demand."

"Did you fight? I thought about you every day of that awful

time, wondering if you were involved in battle."

Light leaped in his eyes. "I wasn't a soldier, but it wasn't always safe working a steamboat."

I shouldn't have betrayed myself so, Libby thought. It had been inappropriate, but she'd spoken without thinking.

"Unlike the railroads, steamboats could often bring needed weapons and ammunition and other supplies almost to the battlefields, if the battlefields were near rivers. We carried so many troops and supplies that many steamboats were attacked. Some were even blown up."

"Yes, I remember."

"Were many local men killed in the war?"

"Too many." She shared with him what had happened to men he'd known, young men with whom they'd gone to school, men she'd socialized with at dances and picnics, men she'd worshipped with in church, men who left on steamboats for Fort Snelling and she'd never seen again, and others who returned home with useless limbs.

Libby brushed her fingertips across her forehead, trying to brush away the memories. "Long after the war, I heard you'd landed in town on a steamboat. Joshua and I had been married for years by then. Still, when I heard you were alive—" She studied his face, reexperiencing the wonder of that day. "I thanked God for keeping you safe through the war."

To her surprise, Spencer looked almost stricken. "It never occurred to me that you would worry so over me. If I'd known, I would have found a way to let you know I was all right."

She pulled her gaze from his. "It's likely better that you didn't." Again she'd spoken beyond the borders of delicacy, but she wasn't sorry. The memories had built up inside her for so many years, with no one with whom to share them! She was fiercely glad she'd been given the opportunity to let him know she'd kept him in her prayers during that awful time.

She watched her fingertip slide gently over the etching on her crystal goblet. "What did you do after the war, Spencer?"

"No one calls me Spencer anymore. My children call me

Father, my grandchildren, Grandfather, and everyone else calls me Captain. I like hearing my name on your lips."

Flustered, Libby couldn't meet his eyes. She was glad he didn't press the sweet talk.

"After the war, steamboats could be had for a song. Still, seemed like a heap of money to me, but I managed to buy a good little boat. It wasn't the best time to be making money steamboating, but I hired the best men I could afford and treated my clients well. Slowly, my business grew into a small packet company. It served me well. Henry and Alexander are running it now."

"I often wondered which boats you captained."

"But you never asked anyone which boats were mine." His voice was low. His gaze kept a firm hold on hers. "Because you couldn't have met my boats at the landing, any more than I could have visited your shop."

Her heart lodged in her throat, beating furiously. She tried to swallow it, gave up, and forced her words around it. "No, I couldn't." She dragged her gaze from his with an effort. "I loved my husband. We had a good life together." It was suddenly terribly important he know that.

"I'm glad, Libby. I always hoped your life was happy. My marriage turned out better than might be expected. Margaret and I were both a bit wild at first, I suppose, but after Henry was born, we settled down. Margaret turned out to be a good mother and faithful wife. Yet I must admit," his voice dropped, taking on a teasing quality, although she heard the seriousness beneath, "I also hoped there would always be a place for me in your heart, as there is for you in mine."

She continued staring at her plate, biting the edge of her lip, thrilling to his words.

"Is there such a place, Libby?"

Slowly, she lifted her eyes to meet his gaze, feeling shy and awkward, and nodded.

His smile made his face look young.

Libby couldn't remember much of the rest of the meal.

Walking home by the mellow light of the gaslights, her arm

tucked securely in his, Libby felt wrapped in intimacy. Their conversation was filled with "Do you remembers." Libby rejoiced in learning which memories of their town and friends and of their times together Spencer had carried in his heart through the years.

When they reached her home, he asked if she wouldn't sit with him in the porch swing awhile. She was thrilled he'd asked, that he wasn't ready to leave her. The spring evening was quite cool, but she didn't want him to think she needed to go inside. She wasn't ready to invite him in to meet Ida, and neither was she ready for him to leave.

A moment later she realized she had nothing to fear on that count. She shivered slightly as she sat down.

"Are you cold, Libby?"

"No."

He sat beside her, slipped his arm around her, and drew her into his embrace. "Is that better?" he whispered, just above her ear.

It was such a delightfully youthful ploy! Libby muffled her laugh against his shoulder.

His broad fingers were warm and firm and gentle beneath her chin, urging her to lift her face. She complied willingly, anticipation tearing away her breath, barely able to see the details of his face in the darkness. Then his lips touched hers, and seeing didn't matter.

His kiss was as familiar as though they had kissed yesterday, tender and warm and sweet and lingering. She gave herself to the beauty and joy of it.

When Spencer finally pulled his lips from hers, it was to whisper, "Ah, Libby, I've missed you so!"

Libby couldn't remember ever being so happy.

His lips touched her brow, her temple, her cheek, leaving warmth in their path. When they reached her lips again, it was many minutes before he released hers.

"I came back to River's Edge because of you, Libby."

Her heart stopped, then barreled on again. "You did?"

"I'd hoped for a glimpse of you, or news of you, at least.

When I heard of your husband's death. . . I'm truly sorry for your loss, but, forgive me, when I heard you were a widow, my heart near leaped from my chest in hope."

She held her breath, waiting for him to continue.

"We've lived more years than we're likely to see again." His arms tightened about her. He rubbed his cheek against her hair, almost dislodging her hat. She didn't mind—enjoyed the closeness. "I've lived without you for thirty-five years. I don't intend to spend the rest of my life without you."

Surely he couldn't be proposing after such short reacquaintance! Libby licked her suddenly dry lips. "What. . .what do you mean?"

His chest moved with his soft chuckle. "Is my intention so obscure? I intend to marry you, Libby."

I'm dreaming. It must be a dream, she thought. His lips, warm against her temple, assured her otherwise. She drew a shaky breath. "I believe your years as a captain have accustomed you to giving orders rather than asking favors. Haven't I anything to say about your intention?"

He again slipped his hand beneath her chin and urged her face upward. His face creased into deep smile wrinkles. "Yes. You can say, 'Yes, I'll spend the rest of my life with you.' "

Her heart yearned to repeat those wonderful words, but her faith and the discipline that was such a part of her came to her rescue. "We can't leap into matrimony without becoming reacquainted."

"There may be details we don't know about each other, but hearts don't change. I know your beautiful heart is the same as when we were young."

"And *your* heart, Spencer. Has it remained the same?" She could barely breathe as she voiced the question she'd been afraid to face. "Or have you come to believe in Christ?"

six

Spencer Matthews's face stiffened. So, Libby was putting God between them again, after all. After the warm, harmonious evening they'd spent together, he'd hoped she'd put aside that silliness. He wished he could ignore her question, but he knew that wasn't possible. "No, I'm not a Christian."

Libby put her hands against his chest and gently pushed herself away, just far enough so she wasn't leaning against him. Fury and frustration raced through him. He grasped her shoulders. "Libby, is it truly important?"

"Yes. Unless we share the same faith, the same love for the Lord—"

"I remember your arguments." His tone, short and curt, made her wince. "I haven't forgotten a word of our last conversation before I left River's Edge."

"I'm sorry. I didn't mean to hurt you." Her voice was so low he could barely hear her.

"Think of the way we fell so easily into comfortable companionship." He leaned toward her. She drew back slightly. He stopped. Pain lanced through him that she would act as though he were repulsive simply because he didn't share her faith. He forced the anger from his voice. "You didn't act as though you believed we were wrong for each other a few minutes ago, before God was mentioned."

"I–I allowed my joy at seeing you to cloud my judgment."

His stomach clenched at her words. "Do you realize how much it hurts to be treated as though you think my embrace is a sin?"

"I'm sorry," she whispered, burying her face in her hands.

He wanted to draw her into his arms once more, but didn't wish to experience the pain of another rebuff. Instead he covered her hands gently with his own. She didn't resist when he

41

took them from her face, though she gasped lightly when he pressed a kiss to her fingers. "I've spent thirty-five years missing you. After this evening, I can't believe you haven't missed me, too."

"I *have* missed you. You've become a permanent part of my heart."

"Then can't we put aside this silly religion talk and believe the love we have for each other, which has lasted through this long separation, will overcome the difference in our faith?"

She didn't answer. He wanted to believe it was because she was trying to convince herself he was right, but he was sure it meant she wouldn't say yes.

He tried another tactic. "If you married me, just think how much time you'd have to try to convert me."

It brought a smile. "If I nagged at you about your faith every day, you'd soon tire of me."

Now he was the one without an answer. Likely he'd find it tedious to deal with the issue daily. "There has to be a way past this stumbling block."

Libby stood, tugging her hands from his. "There is no way around it. It was lovely seeing you again. Thank you, for dinner, and. . .and for letting me know you are alive and well."

"Libby—"

Hearing a sob, he stood and reached for her in one movement. He was too late. His fingertips brushed her short cape as she turned away. She rushed across the porch and through the front door into the small frame home.

Spencer stared at the closed door, unable to comprehend at first that she'd left with no intention of returning. Finally, he stalked down the steps and headed for the hotel.

"This isn't the end, Libby," he muttered. "I've learned a thing or two about getting what I want in life. I want you, and I'm not giving up until you're Mrs. Spencer Matthews."

❧

Libby turned up the flame on the kerosene lamp Ida had left on the table just inside the door. Pressing one hand to her mouth to keep her sobs from waking Ida, she carried the lamp to her bedroom.

She quickly removed her gloves and cape, laying them across the back of a small oak rocking chair. She poured water from the rose-patterned pitcher on her washstand into the matching bowl and splashed the cool water over her face, then dabbed at it with a lavender-scented linen towel.

It didn't help. The tears still came. Libby dropped onto the side of her bed. Crying! She hadn't cried in years, not since the months after Joshua died.

"I've been a fool!" she whispered. "I thought my days of passion were behind me. I'm a mature woman, not an inexperienced girl. How could I have let my guard down, letting him kiss me, with no thought of the consequences?" She groaned and flopped back on the quilt-covered bed. "*Let* him? I welcomed it!"

It had been wonderful. She relived the beauty of the minutes spent in Spencer's arms. With difficulty, she finally pulled her thoughts away. It had felt so right to be in his embrace again, but it hadn't been right. "I guess I wanted those minutes, Lord, wanted those kisses to remember for the rest of my life. It wasn't fair and wasn't wise for either of us. Now I'll likely miss him more than ever."

With a sigh, she went to the bureau and removed her hat, setting it on the lace-covered bureau top. Something caught her eye. She picked up a wooden goose. Holding it in one hand, she stroked its smooth feathers. A moment later, she picked up its twin, remembering Spencer telling her all those years ago that geese mated for life, that he wanted them to spend their lives together forever, too.

When she'd changed into a soft, high-collared flannel nightgown, she moved one of the birds to her nightstand before climbing into the high bed. Sleep didn't come. The evening played itself over and over in her head. "Thank you for giving me this chance to talk with him, Lord, and find out what his life has been like. Please, don't give up on him. Keep working on his heart, so he might know Your dear love and that of Your Son. Not so we can be together. . ." She paused. "Well, that would be nice. No use pretending otherwise when You know my heart better than I do. Still, even if we can never be together, I want him to know the peace and joy of believing in You."

She snuggled her cheek further into her feather pillow. The pillow was soft and comfortable, but she preferred Spencer's shoulder.

A tear slid over her wrinkled cheek and dampened the pillow.

ða

Spencer stalked down the longest dock at the landing, the weathered boards bouncing beneath his feet. At the end of the dock, he sat down, his legs swinging over the water, his hands gripping the dock's rough edge. The current that he knew flowed mightily beneath the smooth, black ribbon of water was nothing compared to the current of anger and despair that stormed through him.

He'd come to the river as he always did when upset, hoping the familiar smells, the regular sound of lapping water, and the moon's wavering gold path would calm him.

He leaned against the large wooden post beside him, letting the evening's events scroll through his mind. Most of it had been wonderful. Just to have the right to sit across from her at a meal, to watch her eyes light up with laughter or soften with a memory, or her gaze skitter away from his when the emotion between them grew intense was a wonder.

His excitement had grown through the evening as he'd realized it truly was the same Libby he'd known all those years ago who looked out from behind the older face. A wiser, more experienced Libby, but the same beautiful spirit. Her spirit had always made her beautiful to him; it always would.

Libby's sweet, lily-of-the-valley scent lingered about him. She'd felt just as he'd remembered in his arms, her kiss was just the same, just as sweet. She'd responded so willingly to his kisses that he'd been certain she'd say yes to his proposal.

"I don't understand how you could say no." He stared at

the water, rippling quietly past, but it was Libby's face he saw, her eyes radiant with what he'd thought was the joy of being together again. "So few lovers are given a second chance. If you have to believe so strongly in God, why can't you believe that He brought us together again, instead of believing He wants to keep us apart?"

In the many times he'd imagined this night through the years, it had never ended this way. Instead, Libby had spoken her love for him and agreed eagerly to spend the rest of their days together as his wife.

He wrapped his arms tightly over his chest, trying to ease the burning ache within. "Oh, Libby, will I ever hold you again?"

❧

Libby managed to eat breakfast with Ida and walk to their business establishments together without mentioning Spencer. Eventually she'd tell Ida everything, but she wasn't ready to yet. It was difficult enough to keep her emotions in check as it was.

In her shop, Libby didn't find it as easy to keep Spencer from her conversations. Every woman who walked through the door had heard of her dinner with Captain Matthews and wanted to know the details.

They didn't hear the details from Libby. No, she assured each one, he's not a suitor, only an old friend. Yes, he had been a steamboat captain. Yes, he does cut a fine figure for a mature gentleman. No, he's not married.

At noon, Libby went into the back room to partake of the simple lunch she'd brought from home, while Miss Silvernail watched the shop. As usual, Ida joined her. She bustled into the back room, her ample hips bouncing, her hat looking as though it would slip from her graying-brown hair any moment.

"Libby Ward, how could you deceive me so?"

"Whatever do you mean?" Libby hoped she appeared innocent. She sat down on the stool behind the worktable and opened her small tin lunch pail.

Ida propped gloved hands on her hips. Her brown eyes flashed. "You know very well what I mean. Who was that man you had dinner with last night? Customers have been asking about you all morning. Between you and the strange lights on the bluff, the women have been so busy prattling that they've barely made a pretense of shopping." She stopped to take a breath, then accused, "I thought you had dinner with the Knights."

"Uh, no, not with the Knights."

"I know that very well now, as does the rest of the town. Who is he?"

"Ida, please sit down. I feel like a wayward child being interrogated by her teacher."

Ida plumped herself down on a wooden work stool.

Libby sighed. Besides, Ida loved anything that hinted of romance. She devoured, not just read, the romantic serials in the newspapers. "I meant to tell you eventually. It was Spencer, Captain Spencer Matthews."

Ida's lips formed an O. Her eyes widened. "The man you turned down when you were just this side of girlhood."

"The same."

Ida leaned forward eagerly. "What is he doing in town? How did you happen to have dinner with him?"

Libby answered in a few short sentences. She didn't tell her of Spencer's marriage proposal. Ida was her best friend, but it was too much to hope Ida could keep such a spicy tidbit from the town's gossip circles.

"Are you going to see him again?"

"I don't think so," Libby admitted. It occurred to her that she didn't even know how long he would be in town.

"But an old beau! It must be a tempting prospect."

Tempting was certainly the right word.

Ida opened her own lunch pail. "If we put our heads together, we can find a way to convince him to escort you again. I know! Why not invite him to the pie supper the Women's Temperance Union is giving Wednesday evening?"

"I've no intention of pursuing him."

Ida gave a snort of disgust. "Anyone would think you weren't interested in marrying again. You won't pursue the captain. You've turned down invitations from all the marriageable men with whom your niece has tried to pair you. I wish I had a niece so concerned with *my* matrimonial status!"

"Would you like me to ask her to arrange a dinner companion for you?" Libby tried to look innocent.

Ida waved a plump finger in front of Libby's nose. "Don't tease me about something as important as a man!" She pulled a sandwich and a piece of cake from her lunch pail. "If you're not interested in the captain, will you introduce me to him?"

Libby only smiled and went back to her lunch.

The afternoon brought more curious friends to the shop. Libby began to wonder whether the local newspaper would insert an item in their social column: "Seen at the River's Edge Hotel Dining Rooms on Tuesday last, Mrs. Libby Ward, proprietor of Mrs. Ward's Fancy Millinery Shop of this town, and Captain Spencer Matthews, distinguished retired steamboat captain and former owner of the Matthews' Packet Company."

She was relieved and pleased to see Constance enter late in the day. "How good to see you, my dear. Are you shopping, or did you stop to say hello while on your other errands?"

"I admit, I only stopped in to see my favorite aunt."

"How nice."

"I've been hearing rumors about you." Constance crossed her arms over her black-and-brown walking suit and gave Libby a look that Libby recognized as a pretense of severity.

Libby straightened the cream-colored silk roses on a blue bonnet's brim. "It's impossible to keep anything in this small town a secret, especially if you're a widow doing something as outrageous as having dinner with a man."

Constance laughed. "At the town's best dining room, with a distinguished gentleman, if the rumors are to be believed. Hardly secretive behavior."

Libby's cheeks warmed. "If we'd had dinner in private, people would have put a nasty complexion on it. As it is, they merely feel free to ask nosey questions." Her shoulders had tightened and her voice grown shrill. She made an effort to relax. "I suppose I shouldn't feel so put out. I've enjoyed gossip as much as the next woman. I even repeat it to my customers, telling myself I'm only carrying on pleasant conversation about friends with my customers. Perhaps this is meant as a lesson to me."

"You never carry malicious gossip. It's only natural to be interested in our friends' and neighbors' lives." Constance leaned against the table. "I'm not going to let you change the subject so easily. Here I've been trying, discreetly, to encourage you to begin seeing someone, and all along you had your eye on someone else."

"That's not exactly the way it was."

"Do I know him?"

Libby shook her head.

"Perhaps I'm leaping to conclusions. As a former Pinkerton agent, I should know better. Is he only a friend?"

"Well. . .he's not a potential beau."

Constance looked disappointed, but she didn't ask any more questions about Spencer. She appeared to be thinking something over, so Libby straightened a display of gloves that the day's clients had mussed and waited for Constance to decide whether to share what was so obviously on her mind.

Finally, Constance took a deep breath and straightened her shoulders. "I fear I owe you an apology."

Libby laughed, honestly surprised. "I hardly think so!"

"Oh, I do. I'm sure you've noticed that there have been other guests lately at a number of the dinners I've invited you to share with us."

Libby pulled a long, white glove through her fingers. "I noticed."

"I did have legitimate social or business reasons to invite each of them," Constance hurriedly assured her, "but I admit I've tried to play matchmaker." Her shoulders slumped. "I shouldn't have interfered in your life that way. It's just that I'm so happy with Justin. I want you to have someone with whom to share that special kind of love."

"I knew that was the reason behind your invitations to the unmarried men."

"It was meddlesome."

"Yes, but I knew it was done in love, so it was easy to overlook."

"Thank you." Constance lifted her shoulders in a shrug. "I make an awful matchmaker, anyway. How could I have thought for a moment of exposing you to an evening in Mr. Copperfield's company?"

They laughed together at the memory of the stern, pinch-nosed schoolteacher who had been one of the male dinner guests.

"I have to admit," Constance began, "I did think something might grow between you and Pastor Green. You seemed so comfortable together."

"Most of the men you arranged for my dinner companions were nice men, Constance, but Joshua and I had a wonderful marriage. I'm not willing to accept any man into my life just to be married again." It was only part of the truth. She wanted to tell Constance about Spencer's place in her heart, the place he continued to fill, even though there was no hope they could share a future. She searched her mind for the right words and her heart for the courage.

Constance picked up a small black purse covered with jet beads from the display behind them and played with it idly. She caught her bottom lip between her teeth, then released it and rushed in. "Don't you ever get tired of life's struggles? Don't you wish sometimes there were someone there to share the load, help with money, make some of your decisions for you, that sort of thing?"

"Humph!" Libby jerked her chin into the air. "Of course I do. I'm human, aren't I?" She pounded an index finger in a rapid staccato on the oak display table. "But whenever I start feeling those collywobbles, I remind myself of the married women I know who can't spend a penny or attend a church social without their husband's approval. Then I hie myself up and get busy putting together a new bonnet or scrubbing the kitchen floor or making a cake for a busy young mother." She shook her head vigorously. "There are worse things in life for a woman than supporting herself."

Constance's eyes sparkled with laughter. "I should have realized you didn't need and wouldn't appreciate my help in deciding whether to bring a man into your life, let alone in choosing one. You run your life so capably."

Libby stared at her, pleased. "Do you think so?"

"Of course." Constance made a sweeping motion with one arm. "Look how well you run this store. The women think you're a wonder when it comes to creating hats and keeping them in fashion. And don't think I've forgotten that you intended to raise Effie and Evan after their parents died. That's why I first came to River's Edge, to bring the children to you from Chicago. If I hadn't met Justin on the train and married him, you'd be raising them now, and doing a wonderful job of it, I'm sure. Oh, yes, Aunt Libby, you're a strong woman."

"Other people have said that. I don't feel strong." She shrugged. "Difficult times come into everyone's lives. The longer one lives, the more of them one experiences. The way I see it, when things seem overwhelming, there are only two choices: give up or keep on going. If one gives up, there isn't any hope for a brighter future. What is strong, then, about choosing to keep going? What is there to do but keep going?"

"Sometimes putting one step in front of the other to keep going takes all the strength one has."

"Life hands everyone material with which to create their lives. No use complaining if you receive calico while another receives silk. You make do with what you have. Some mighty pretty gowns can be made from calico, and they're much more practical than ones made from silk, if I do say so, loving beautiful clothes as I do."

Her words to Constance about not needing a man to support her or lean on were true, but how did a woman stop longing for the arms of a man she loved or wanting more than anything to share his life? She was well aware not all women had the resources to support themselves as she did and understood that it was for that reason society found it acceptable for women to remarry late in life. *Women at my age are expected to act mature, not giddy with love like a young woman.*

She lifted her chin, suddenly determined to get past her embarrassment and tell Constance about her girlish infatuation with Spencer. "There's something I want to tell you—"

The door opened to the usual accompaniment of the bells and sounds of the trolley and horses and wagons in the street. Libby's hand flew to her throat. *Spencer!*

Their gazes met across the room and held. Then Spencer turned away, pulling off his hat. He stopped in front of a display of leghorn bonnets trimmed with ostrich feathers, looking as though he was considering a purchase.

Constance's eyes danced. "I'd best leave and let you wait on your customer."

"He isn't a customer. He's the gentleman with whom I dined last evening." Libby took her hand. "Come. I'd like you to meet him."

They stopped across the table from Spencer. He looked up, waiting for Libby to speak.

"This is Mrs. Justin Knight, the niece of whom I've told you. Constance, this is Captain Spencer Matthews."

Spencer bowed slightly from the waist. "Mrs. Knight. It is indeed a pleasure to meet you."

Constance smiled warmly. "And you, Captain." Her gaze swept his coat and the braid-trimmed hat in his hand. "I assume you captain a steamboat?"

His gaze darted to Libby. She shifted slightly in discomfort. *He's thinking I haven't told Constance about him,* she realized.

"Yes. Retired," he answered.

"Will you be staying in River's Edge long?" Constance asked.

He glanced at Libby, then back at Constance. "I'm not certain. I've some business to transact. I'll be staying until the contract is signed."

Does he truly have business, or is he referring to a marriage contract? Libby wondered.

"My husband owns the local bank," Constance was telling him. "I'm certain he'd be glad to assist you if there's anything he might do to help you conclude your business successfully."

"That's a mighty kind offer, Mrs. Knight." He beamed. Shifted his gaze to Libby. "Isn't it?" His smile grew larger.

Marriage contract, Libby decided, her heart quivering. "Very kind. However, I doubt Justin will be able to help with the type of business which you have in mind."

Constance glanced from one to another uncertainly. "I'd best be going. I left Effie and Evan at Perkins' General Store. No telling what mischief they've gotten into by this time. Good day, Captain." She kissed Libby lightly on the cheek. "I'll talk with you later."

Libby's heart started beating faster as Constance left her alone with Spencer. Why had he come?

She hadn't long to wonder.

"Will you have dinner with me again this evening, Libby?"

seven

Libby pressed her lips together hard. She hadn't thought Spencer would come around again! Now that the opportunity was before her, she wanted desperately to spend another evening with him. *Didn't you learn anything last night? Where could another evening with him lead but to more misery?* she warned herself.

She took a deep breath. "I don't think that would be wise, Spencer." It wasn't exactly a no, she realized, berating herself for her weakness.

His eyes darkened. "What harm could come from sharing a meal?"

She didn't answer. It wasn't the meal that worried her.

"I want to see you again, Libby. There's so much we haven't discussed. Have dinner with me, as friends."

She spread her hands. "You don't wish to be only friends, and there's nowhere beyond that for our relationship to grow."

"Last night left me with the impression I'm not the only one who wants more than friendship between us."

"I told you—"

"I'm not thinking of your words, but of your actions."

Libby looked away in embarrassment.

"Caring for each other is not something of which to be ashamed." His voice was low, almost pleading.

"I'm not ashamed of the. . .caring. It isn't wise to act on our feelings when we can have no future together."

He placed his large palms on the table and leaned toward her. "That isn't an ending that's written in blood. You can decide otherwise."

Libby linked her fingers together in front of her and forced herself to look him squarely in the eyes. Would he notice her chin trembling? "I've *chosen* to decide we cannot have a future together if we do not love and follow the same God."

Spencer glared at her. He whipped around. His boots clipped smartly against the wooden floor. He didn't turn for a last look as he went out the door.

Libby shook all over with the effort it took to keep from running after him. Was this the last time she'd see him; his back to her, walking away in anger, the same way he'd left her thirty-five years ago? *Is that why You brought him back, Lord? So I would live through this all over again?*

Shame instantly dampened her self-pity. She'd been thankful God had let her know Spencer was still alive. She was no less thankful for that now, in spite of the pain she was reliving. "Help me trust You, Lord."

&

Captain Spencer Matthews stormed past the quiet business establishments, dodging townspeople on the boardwalk. If some of them remarked on his pushy manner or looked askance at him, he didn't notice.

Fury at his helplessness poured through his veins like liquid fire. Libby wasn't giving them a chance, and there wasn't a thing he could do about it.

He headed for the landing. He wanted to be alone, where he could think. *If there's anything I've learned in life, it's that anything is possible.* Hadn't being a steamboat captain only been a dream at one time? And owning a steamboat? Now his packet company owned several. *To win Libby over, I just need a plan.*

Ideas always came easier to him on the river. He stopped at a small frame building at the landing to rent a rowboat.

The wiry man of about thirty with dark hair and a short, scraggly beard named the price, then leaned his elbows on the wooden counter while Spencer dug out his money. "You the retired steamboat captain I been hearin' is in town?"

Spencer nodded sharply. "Guess that must be me."

"I'm a steamboat man myself. Name's Adams. 'Course, I'm not a captain." The man grinned lazily. "I'm just fillin' in time, workin' here on the docks. Me and my pal took a trip up here to visit friends. We planned to catch the paddle wheeler we work on, the *Spartan,* when it made its first trip north for the year."

Spencer laid a bill on the counter. "Thought I heard the *Spartan* hit a snag down near New Orleans and was laid up for repairs."

"Yep. So my pal and me are still waitin'."

"Too bad. Maybe you can get work on another steamboat until the *Spartan*'s ready. Always work available for experienced men."

"Think we'll wait around these parts till our boat's ready. We're pretty fond of the *Spartan*."

"May I have my change?" He was beginning to feel all too conspicuous in the small town to which he'd been so eager to return. He was accustomed to passengers telling him their life story, but not strangers on land. Right now, he was in no mood for small talk.

Relief settled over him as he stepped into the rowboat. The hotel clerk had told him this morning about a steamboat that had run aground upstream a month ago, right after the ice went out on the river. It was still there. He was curious to see it. He might as well head in that direction now.

Rowing was more work than he'd remembered, but he enjoyed the challenge. It helped cool his anger to spend his energy physically. The familiar sound of water lapping against the boat, the gentle rocking, and the fishy odor of river water all helped calm him.

He was soon beyond River's Edge. Bluffs, dense with spring-greening trees at their base and majestic with sheer limestone cliffs on top, bordered his water road. While he rowed, he studied his problem.

The first step in trying to solve a problem, he'd learned, was identifying it, stating it clearly. "The problem is Libby's refusal to accept me unless I become a Christian," he told a gull that landed on the stern.

The gull lifted its wings and let out a raucous cry, then settled down to fix him with its beady stare.

Spencer repeated the problem out loud. "So the solution is to change Libby's mind." He grimaced. "That should be easy. About like pushing a steamboat upstream by hand." One thing about Libby, it was always a challenge trying to change her mind about anything.

Memories of friendly debates they'd had as children drifted through his mind, bringing a smile, but no solution.

"Okay, Captain, start again." He heaved a sigh, dug the oars deeply into the muddy water, and repeated the problem slowly. "The problem is Libby's refusal to accept me unless I become a Christian."

He stopped rowing, his hands resting on the oars. "Unless." Was that word the key?

He shook his head hard. It wasn't like a man could create faith in God just by deciding to do so. "But maybe I don't have to create faith. Wouldn't hurt me any to become a regular churchgoer. Might be hard to keep my skepticism to myself and listen to some of those sermons, but if it meant Libby would let me court her, it would be worth it."

He dipped the oars into the water once more. After all, how hard could it be to pretend to be a Christian? Follow the Ten Commandments. He did that anyway, for the most part, all except that first one. How did it go again? He couldn't remember exactly, something about believing in God, or trusting Him, or honoring Him. If a man went to church and kept the rest of the commandments, who would know if he followed the first one?

His plan began to form. He'd begin attending church this Sunday. Might even join Sunday school. Ask the pastor about joining the church.

It wasn't as if he hadn't set foot inside a church since he'd left River's Edge. Margaret had convinced him their boys needed to be brought up attending church. He'd grudgingly agreed. At least the church would give the boys a moral compass. On the rare Sundays he was at home instead of on the river, he'd attended with the family, though in so doing he felt a hypocrite.

Let's see. Step Two. He'd have to settle in River's Edge for a while if he planned to win Libby back. And he intended to win her back, no matter how long it took. Nothing he had to be back in St. Louis for, anyway. His boys were handling the family steamboat company admirably.

He'd get to know Libby's friends, join in social engagements where she'd be present. No doubt that would include a lot of church socials. He chuckled. At least the food was usually good at those events.

Having a plan lightened his heart. He threw his weight into the rowing and belted out a river song he'd learned in his early days of river boating to the accompaniment of creaking oars. The song carried across the water to the bluffs on either side of the river and bounced back to him:

> *Timber don't get too heavy for me,*
> *And sacks too heavy to stack,*
> *All that I crave for many a long day,*
> *Is your loving when I get back.*
> *I'm working my way back home.*

> *Now Paducah's laying 'round the bend,*
> *Now Paducah's laying 'round the bend,*
> *Captain, don't whistle, just ring your bell,*
> *For my woman'll be standing right there.*
> *I'm working my way back home.*

As he finished the song, he rounded a bend and spotted the steamboat, stranded on a sandbar far to the side of the main channel.

He shook his head. He knew firsthand how treacherous it was to navigate a river. A good pilot, familiar with the river's bends and twists and shallows, was more valuable than gold to a steamboat captain. His own favorite pilot hated the stretch of the Upper Mississippi between Minnesota and Wisconsin. "During low water," he used to say, "my paddle wheels raise clouds of dust."

"Water's not too low this time of year," the captain muttered. Winter runoff always caused spring flooding, with the resultant high water. Invariably, it also changed the river's bottom. "Must have been what happened here. Channel changed since the pilot's last run, and his charts weren't current. The hotel clerk said the boat ran aground at night."

The usual attempts to grasshopper the boat over the bar with spars and derricks hadn't worked. The boat hadn't been carrying much of a load, so even after the cargo was unloaded with the assistance of dockhands from River's Edge, the boat hadn't risen far enough to free it. Some tugboats had been sent out from River's Edge to try to pull the steamboat off the bar, without success. The next day, the captain, who'd owned the boat, died.

Likely if the boat had been owned by a packet company, as so many were, the owners would have continued attempts to free the boat. As it was, the townspeople decided to wait, hoping spring rains would raise the water level enough to float or pull the boat off the bar. So far, that hadn't happened. If it didn't happen soon, they'd try using hoses to wash out the mud beneath the boat.

"At least the boat's bottom can't be damaged too badly. If it were, the back end of the boat would have sunk to the bottom by now."

Spencer nosed his boat up beside the steamboat, watching for the sandbar. He could just make out the top of the bar beneath Big Muddy's waters. It was too low, however, to beach his rowboat on it.

He rowed around the boat, examining it. It was an older stern-wheeler, badly in need of fresh paint. The boat was small compared to some of the elegant steamers. There were only two decks below the texas, where the captain and other officers' cabins were located, and the pilothouse that topped the boat like the top tier of a cake. "Jennie Lee" was painted in bold black letters along the side of the pilothouse. He recognized the name of the inauspicious boat. Every captain worth his salt knew the names of all the steamboats that plied the same rivers as his own boats.

Spencer headed around the back of the boat, circling the paddle wheel. "What the—"

A rope hung from the wheel, its end drifting in the water.

Spencer rowed closer. *Maybe the rope was left by people trying to free the boat.* But when he examined the rope, he could tell it hadn't been in the river that long.

Using the rope to secure his boat, he scrambled onto the paddle wheel. Grunting, he finally made it to the lower deck. "Never was my favorite way to board a steamer," he muttered, wiping his hands on his trousers.

He walked past the boiler room and along the empty cargo deck toward the bow. Locating a stairway, he climbed to the second deck. He opened a couple stateroom doors for quick looks inside.

He swung open the double doors to the dining hall and snorted in disgust. The furnishings, obviously once fine, were shabby. Brass trimmings were tarnished with age. The draperies were almost transparent from sun damage. The boat was old, but that was no reason to let it fall into this kind of shape.

Letting the doors swing shut, he mounted another flight of stairs. The captain's safe was usually kept in the captain's quarters in the texas.

He opened the door to the captain's quarters. His gaze swept the richly paneled room. A large, round, walnut desk stood in the middle of the room. Behind it, two brown-haired children, a boy and a girl, obviously brother and sister, about eight years old, stared at him with huge eyes.

The captain's jaw dropped.

The children's jaws trembled.

The girl summoned her courage. "Are. . .are you a ghost, mister?"

eight

"A ghost?" The words exploded from Spencer's mouth. "Of course not! What kind of fool question is that?"

The girl's knuckles, gripping the edge of the table, were white. "W–well, you're dressed like a captain, and the captain died on this ship."

"It's a b–boat, Ef–Effie," the boy corrected her, never taking his gaze from Spencer.

Why, they're terrified of me, Spencer realized. He sat down and forced his voice to sound calm. "I'm Captain Spencer Matthews. I was a steamboat captain, but—"

"W–was?" Effie asked. "B–before you died?"

"Of course not!"

Effie took a step backward, landing her against the wall. The boy followed.

Spencer swallowed hard. "I'm not dead. I've never been on this ship before, alive or dead."

"P–promise?" the boy whispered.

Spencer laid a hand over his heart. "Promise."

"How did you get here if you're not a ghost?" Effie asked.

"I have a rowboat tied up at the paddle wheel." He saw the girl begin to visibly relax, her shoulders lowering half an inch. "How did you two get here?"

It was Effie who answered. "We found a log washed up against the shore. We pushed it into the water and laid on top of it, paddling with our hands until we got out here."

Spencer felt his face drain of blood. "Don't you know how dangerous that was? You could have drowned!"

"We didn't. Anyway, you can't boss us around."

He ignored that. At least Effie must be losing her fear of him if she could talk back in that sassy manner. "Did you tie the rope to the paddle wheel?"

They nodded.

"Where did you get the rope?"

"We brought it from home," the boy answered. "Because the first time we saw the boat, we couldn't find a way to get out to it."

Effie nodded. "We tied the rope to a branch on our log, so we could get back to shore."

"But the branch broke," the boy interrupted, "and the log floated away, so we're stuck here."

Spencer was glad to see the thought of being stranded was beginning to frighten the boy more than the idea that Spencer might be a ghost. "I'll take you to shore in my rowboat."

Neither of them looked very comforted by his offer.

"Where do you two live?"

"River's Edge."

"What are your names?"

They didn't answer.

He smiled. "I told you my name." He looked at the girl. "I heard your brother call you Effie."

Her eyes widened again. "How do you know he's my brother?"

"I'm guessing. You two couldn't look more alike if you were twins."

"We *are* twins," the boy said. "My name is Evan."

"Effie and Evan." Spencer grinned. "I should have known. Libby told me all about you."

"You know Aunt Libby?" Evan asked.

Spencer nodded. "I knew her long before either of you were born. I lived in River's Edge then." He recalled the stories Libby had told him about the children. "Were you playing detective when you boarded the boat?"

Effie's eyes flashed. She planted her hands on her hips. "We don't *play* detective, we *practice* detecting!"

Spencer wiped a hand over his mouth and beard, trying to wipe away his grin. "Sorry. My mistake."

"You needn't laugh!" Effie stomped her foot. It made an ineffectual "thud" on the wooden floor. "We've helped Aunt

Constance find criminals before."

"Aunt Constance was a Pinkerton before she married Uncle Justin." Evan's voice was thick with pride.

"One of the criminals Aunt Constance caught was a real mean man named Rasmus Pierce." Effie hunched her shoulders, narrowed her eyes, and screwed up her round face in an attempt to look tough. "He hid money he stole from a train in some caves in the bluffs."

"So your aunt Libby told me." Spencer crossed his arms over his chest. "Did you find any clues to a crime on board?"

"We aren't trying to solve a crime on the ship," Effie told him.

"Boat," Evan corrected again. "We want to find out about the lights in the cliff."

"Oh, yes." Spencer nodded. "I heard about them in town. Isn't it hard to see the lights during the day?"

"We figured the ghost wouldn't be out in the daytime," Effie explained reasonably.

"But when we got here, we saw the log," Evan said, "so we decided to explore the boat first."

"And then we got stuck here," Effie finished.

"I see. Well," he pushed himself to his feet, "I think we'd better head back to town. It's going to be dark soon, and your family will be worried about you."

The bluffs cut off the lowering sun's last rays, casting shadow along the path of the three traveling the river back to town. The children huddled together on one seat beneath Spencer's coat while the captain rowed. His muscles complained of the unexpected strain of two long rowings in one day, and he was thankful the trip back was with the current.

Once in River's Edge, Spencer walked the children to their home in the most elegant part of town. The frame house was a huge example of all the curves and curlicues of Victorian architecture, set on a large lot.

He reached for the brass knocker on the front door. Before he could grasp it, Evan had the door open. Uncomfortable at the idea of walking into a stranger's home without an invitation from the adult owners, Spencer stood uncertainly while the children entered, but only for a moment. Effie looked back at him from the other side of the threshold. "Come on." She grabbed his hand and tugged.

Her sweet gesture caused his tough old heart to twinge. They stepped inside together.

Although he'd already made note of the elite neighborhood, the elegance of the home startled him. The hallway was wide, paneled in walnut. A stairway, with a fine Oriental carpet quieting treads, curved upward at one side. The ceiling, two stories above, was covered with a mural of sky and clouds and cherubs and edged with gilt.

It took only a moment to take everything in, which was all the time he had. Libby and Constance rushed into the hall between two large open doors from the parlor.

Constance dropped to her knees, sweeping the children into her embrace. "Thank God, you're safe!"

The children hugged her, then leaned back in the arms that still circled them. "Of course, we're safe," Effie assured.

Evan nodded vigorously.

Libby stood behind Constance, her hands gripped together. Her gaze met Spencer's. In it he read questions, relief, and gratitude. He smiled, hoping to reassure her that all was indeed well.

Constance wiped a tear from her cheek, stood up, and crossed her arms. "Where have you been?"

Effie shrugged. "Playing."

Evan nodded again.

Constance glared at them with the frustrated concern Spencer recognized from similar events with his own boys. "Do you realize we've scoured the town for you? Justin and the stable boy and neighbors are still looking for you."

"We're sorry." Effie clasped her hands behind her back and watched the toe of her shoe as she dragged it back and forth on the carpet.

"Where were you?"

"Detecting," Evan answered.

Constance shook her head. "You know your uncle Justin

doesn't want you playing detective. Where were you 'detectiving' that you were unable to get home in time for dinner?"

Effie pressed her lips together, still watching the toe of her shoe. Evan watched her shoe, too. *Guilt is written all over them,* Spencer thought, yet he didn't feel it was his place to make their explanations, at least not unless he was asked to do so.

He noticed Libby was looking more worried as the children's obvious sidestepping continued. The thought flashed through his mind, *What would it have been like to raise children with her? How would the two of us have handled together the everyday challenges of child raising?*

"Well?" Constance demanded.

"We were detectiving by the river," Evan muttered.

"The river?" Color drained from Constance's face. "After all the warnings you've had against playing there?"

"We were careful," Effie insisted. "Can't you tell? We're fine."

"The riverbank is not a play area, especially at night." Constance wagged a finger in front of their faces. "I don't want to hear of you going anywhere near the river, ever again, without an adult. Do you hear me?"

The children nodded, staring at Constance wide-eyed. Spencer remembered Libby telling him of Constance's serene nature. He wondered whether she'd ever before spoken to the children this sharply.

"Spencer," Libby said, standing beside Constance, "how did you happen to bring the children home?"

"We met on the river."

Libby spread her hands, looking confused. "How did you know who they were?"

"We introduced ourselves." He wasn't certain how much to reveal. *It's important Mrs. Knight know the risks the children took today, but I'd rather the children told her.*

Now Constance was looking at him curiously, her head tilted to one side. "At the landing?"

"No, ma'am." He hesitated, watching the children. They

were watching him, their gazes wide and anxious. He lifted his eyebrows. "Do you want to tell her, or should I?"

Effie heaved a sigh, lifted her arms from her sides, and let them drop back. "I guess I will."

Spencer smiled at her encouragingly. He well remembered from his own youth the terrors of revealing the tasting of forbidden pleasures.

Effie turned back to Constance. "We wanted to do some detectiving about the ghost and the lights on the bluffs."

"You remember," Evan interrupted. "The ghost of the steamboat captain."

Constance tapped her fingers against her arm. "I remember."

"Anyway," Effie continued, "we went to the bluffs. But then we decided maybe we should look for clues on the steamboat first."

Libby lifted her fingers to her mouth. "Oh, my!"

"That's where we met Captain Matthews, on the steamboat," Effie concluded. "Then he took us home in his rowboat."

Spencer almost chuckled. What a master of deception! She'd managed to tell the truth without telling the whole truth and without lying.

Constance looked at Spencer. "Is that all?"

He clasped his hands behind his back and rocked back on his heels. "I think the question you need to ask next is, how did they get out to the steamboat?"

Effie snorted and crossed her arms over her chest. "Oh, all right! We paddled out on a log."

Constance sat down hard on a hall chair. Her face went white.

Libby grabbed the back of the chair with one hand and rested the other on Constance's shoulder. "You could have drowned!"

"We didn't," Evan reminded his aunts.

Constance took a deep breath. Spencer could see her struggling to regain control.

The front door opened, and a man walked in. His face was the picture of despair and fear. Spencer realized immediately he must be Justin Knight. He was about five feet, eight inches, with broad shoulders and wavy brown hair. He looked vaguely familiar.

Justin glanced at Spencer in surprise, then turned his attention to the children. Relief washed his features with joy. He dropped to his knees, held out his arms, and the children rushed into them.

Then the story had to be told again. Constance repeated most of it. By the end, Justin looked grim, and Spencer expected the children would receive a tongue-lashing and strict punishment before the evening was over.

Deciding he had more than overstayed his welcome, Spencer moved toward the door, thinking to slip away without being noticed.

"You wouldn't leave without allowing me a chance to thank you, sir, surely." Justin crossed the hallway with his hand extended.

Spencer took it. "I only did what any other man would do." He leaned forward so his voice wouldn't carry to the children. "If I might be so intrusive, I suggest you keep in mind your own youthful escapades in determining their punishment."

Justin looked startled. Then he grinned a bit sheepishly. "I'll do that, sir."

"Is your father by any chance Albert Knight? You're the spitting image of him."

"Yes, he's my father. Did you know him?"

Spencer laughed. "Did I! You might ask him about some of our early adventures together."

"I wish I could. He's been dead a number of years now. Mother, too."

"I'm sorry." Spencer felt that wave of loss he always felt when he heard of the death of someone he'd known. "I haven't seen him since I left River's Edge as a young man, but I have fond memories of him."

"Thank you." Justin laid a hand on Spencer's shoulder. "If you're going to be in River's Edge for a few days, I hope you'll have dinner with us one night. I'd love to hear some of your stories about Father."

Spencer couldn't keep from darting a grin at Libby. "Thank you, Mr. Knight. I'll take you up on that offer." *Things couldn't have worked out better,* he thought. *This is the only family Libby has left. She can't avoid me if I become friends with them.* He was sure he'd enjoy each of them even if it weren't for Libby, but he recognized a gift when he saw one.

The encouraging turn of events made him bold. "Mrs. Ward, if you're planning to leave soon, I'd be honored to escort you home."

He noticed the way her lips pressed hard together, and the amused look Constance gave her, before she finally agreed to his offer.

Things didn't continue as well as he'd hoped. Libby had little to say on the walk home, although the way was quite long. They passed from the elite neighborhood to an older neighborhood with simpler homes.

At her home, she climbed the two wooden steps to the porch, then turned to face him. They were almost the same height now. "Thank you, Spencer, for bringing the children home. You. . .you may have saved their lives."

He heard a stifled sob in her voice and laid a hand on her arm. It was true; he may have saved their lives. No telling what would have happened if the children had tried to get back to shore by themselves. Still, he didn't want to frighten Libby further. "They're good kids."

"I think God brought you to that steamboat at just the time you were needed. Don't you, Spencer?"

"Maybe."

Libby smiled, evidently pleased at his admission of the possibility. "Good night."

Wouldn't you know, he thought, disgusted, as he left. *I bring the kids home, and she gives God the credit!*

nine

Sunday morning Libby took her usual place in church, third pew from the front, with Constance's family. "I enter church at the end of a hectic week feeling like a dusty, battered old hat," she'd once told Constance, "and leave feeling clean, newly blocked, with fresh trimmings, ready to face the world again."

This morning more than usual she'd come seeking renewed strength, but her mind strayed constantly to Spencer and memories of Sundays when they were young. In spite of his disbelief, he'd attended church regularly out of respect for his parents' faith. The town had been younger than she and Spencer, and the church had been the center of social as well as spiritual life.

His parents were sincere Christians, Lord, she prayed silently. *I know they tried to bring Spencer up to love You. Why didn't they succeed?*

Libby felt a tug at her sleeve. With a start, she realized everyone was standing. Effie was trying to balance the small hymnbook open in one hand while urging Libby to stand with the other. Libby hurried to oblige her.

Effie looked around restlessly while they waited to begin singing. Suddenly her freckled face lit up with a smile, and she gave someone a discreet wiggle-her-fingers wave.

Libby glanced over her shoulder to see who had caught her attention. *Spencer!*

She stumbled over the words of the hymn, causing Effie to glance at her curiously. She barely heard the preacher speak the words of the final blessing that always added special peace to her spirit as she left the service.

Libby fiddled with her pocketbook while people filed from their pews. The Knight family made their way into the aisle, exchanging greetings with friends.

"Captain Matthews! Wait!"

Libby looked up at Effie's call and saw Effie and Evan wiggling through the slow-moving church members to reach Spencer.

Constance stopped at the end of the pew. "Aren't you coming?"

Libby forced a smile and joined her. As they started down the aisle, women and children stopped constantly to smile at Maria Louise or chuck her under the chin and croon, "She is so-o-o cute."

Libby glanced down the aisle. *Oh, no,* she thought. Spencer stood at the end of a pew, just off the aisle, a few rows down. The children were chattering away with him, and Justin had stopped to greet him. *I won't have any choice but to speak with him. If I don't, Constance will surely ask why I've ignored him.*

Her heartbeat quickened as they approached Spencer. He looked distinguished in his suit, his hair and beard neatly trimmed. She noticed other women their age casting curious looks his way.

Her thoughts were a jumble of questions. *What is he doing here? Is he here to see me? I'm sure he hasn't become a Christian since last evening!*

"I hope you'll join us for the men's Bible study classes," Justin was saying to Spencer when Libby and Constance reached them.

"Thank you, I will." Spencer looked past Justin's shoulder and smiled at Libby. "You're looking especially lovely this morning, Mrs. Ward."

Libby's heart dropped to her stomach and bounced back to her chest. Her shoulders tightened, and her fingers clenched her pocketbook tightly, as if her body were bracing to protect her emotions from him. "Thank you." Her voice sounded stiff.

A moment before, she'd wanted to ignore him. Now she was perversely glad she'd worn her new spring outfit. A tiny turquoise blue bow topped the small silk jabot at her neck, and a large, jaunty bow of the same turquoise was tied at the cream-colored gown's waist.

Spencer turned his attention back to Justin. "I'll stop at the bank tomorrow morning, then, to discuss the purchase."

Libby's cheeks warmed. She felt as though she'd been rebuffed. *Quit acting like a silly schoolgirl,* she scolded herself. *No reason he should give you all his attention. Besides, didn't you tell him you didn't want to see him?*

"Now that you'll be living here," Justin was saying, "you'll have to come for that dinner we talked about."

His words hit Libby like a bolt of lightning. "Living here?"

Justin rested a hand on Spencer's shoulder. "The captain is buying the beached steamboat. He plans to live on it while he refurbishes it."

Spencer's eyes danced with fun and challenge as they met Libby's.

Libby's knees felt like melted butter. She grabbed the edge of the pew back beside her with one hand.

"Oh, boy!" Effie jumped up and down, the huge white collar on her robin's-egg-blue silk dress moving up and down, too, like a graceful white wave beneath her long brown curls.

"That's great." Evan climbed up on the pew while he spoke, so he could get closer to Spencer. "Can we visit you on the steamboat?"

"Yes, can we?" Effie seconded.

"Children, where are your manners?" Constance reproved mildly.

"I mean, *please,* can we?" Effie corrected.

Constance shifted Maria Louise to one hip, slipped a hand over one of Effie's shoulders, and pulled Effie gently back against her skirt. "It isn't polite to invite yourself to visit a busy man like Captain Matthews."

"On the contrary, I consider it a compliment that this pair of fine youngsters would like to spend time with an old codger like me."

Libby's heart warmed at his words, but her knees were still trying to recover from the news that he would be living in River's Edge.

Constance's smile showed her pleasure at his kindness toward the twins. "Perhaps we can arrange a time for them to visit you when you come to dinner. Would this evening be convenient?"

"Can't think of anything I'd rather do tonight, ma'am."

"Good. Will you join us, Libby?"

Libby blinked, startled. She should have expected the invitation. After all, she'd been the one to introduce Constance to Spencer. She didn't have the emotional strength to spend an evening in his company, even with the Knights. "Ida and I plan to dine together." It was a weak excuse, but all her brain could invent on a moment's notice.

Constance's green eyes narrowed slightly, but to Libby's relief, she didn't comment.

Spencer winked at Maria Louise. The little girl giggled, her face alive with laughter. "I have a granddaughter your daughter's age, Mrs. Knight."

"Would you like to hold her?"

Delight spread over Spencer's wide, rugged face. "May I?"

Maria Louise leaned toward him, holding out her arms with a baby's simple, straightforward trust.

Does that trust touch adults so because we've all lost the ability to trust completely through the years and long for it back? Libby mused.

Maria Louise appeared perfectly content in Spencer's strong arms. She poked a finger into his beard, staring curiously at the place her fingertip disappeared.

Even as she laughed, Libby's heart swelled with pain. It looked so natural, Spencer holding a child against his chest, his craggy, worn face so close to the fresh, new one, his attention completely taken up in her. In that moment, she glimpsed in the man she loved the father she'd never seen in him as a young man. *Thank You, Lord, for this memory. I'll always treasure it.*

He was reluctantly handing Maria Louise back to Constance when Pastor Green came up the aisle from the door, where he'd been greeting members as they left, and stopped beside Libby.

Justin introduced him to Spencer.

"Welcome to our church, Captain." Pastor Green reached to shake hands with Spencer. "I hope you'll join us again."

"I'll be living here for a while. You can expect to see me every Sunday."

Pastor Green beamed. "That's good news."

Warning bells went off in Libby's head. What was Spencer doing, saying he would be in church every Sunday and agreeing to attend the men's Bible study?

"Mrs. Ward, may I speak with you a moment?"

"Of course." She allowed the pastor to take her elbow and lead her a few feet away.

He came right to the point. "The Women's Temperance League is having a pie supper Wednesday night to raise money for their cause. Would you allow me to escort you?"

Her first inclination was to say no. He was a nice man, but she felt no attraction to him. He was one of the men with whom Constance had paired her at dinner, the one whom Constance had felt most certain would attract Libby. Libby had been relieved when he hadn't followed up the dinner with an invitation.

From the corner of her eye, she saw Spencer watching her. Perhaps if she appeared to welcome another man's attentions, Spencer would quit trying to talk her into marriage.

"I'd enjoy attending the dinner with you, Pastor." Even if she wasn't interested in a romantic relationship with him, she was sure he'd be a pleasant companion for the evening.

A grin split his smooth, slender face. "Wonderful! Shall I stop for you at six?"

When she rejoined the Knights, Constance whispered, "I couldn't help overhearing. Are you going to the WCTU dinner with him?"

Spencer turned from chattering Effie to stare at Libby.

He heard, she thought. She hesitated in answering Constance. She wanted to discourage Spencer's attentions, yet she hated hurting him. Finally, she nodded.

Constance squeezed her arm. "I'm so pleased. He's a very kind man."

"Yes, he is." Libby suddenly and nonsensically wanted to cry.

Spencer frowned. Libby thought she saw a shadow cross his eyes. She wanted to reach out to him, to ask him to forgive her for allowing another man to court her.

Mentally, she shook herself. Wasn't this the reason she'd accepted Pastor Green's invitation, to discourage Spencer? So why did she feel so awful?

When they left the church, they found a number of people in informal groups on the lawn, visiting in the spring sunshine. Libby heard the words *bluffs, lights, dead captain,* and *ghost* repeatedly. The mystery was still the talk of the town.

Mr. Copperfield, the unpleasant, pinch-nosed schoolteacher who had been one of Constance's dinner guests, broke away from three other men and made his way to them. He greeted Libby and the Knights. After he and Spencer were introduced and shook hands, Copperfield pressed his thin lips together in the manner Libby recognized meant someone had breached his list of do's and don'ts. Immediately she scolded herself. The man's ethics and morals appeared high, as they should be, especially for a teacher and leader of children. It was only his attitude of self-appointed judge that she found distasteful.

"A number of church members are planning an outing this evening to the bluffs." Copperfield's voice dripped disapproval. "Carriage rides to see ghosts are hardly appropriate entertainment for Christians."

With an effort, Libby pushed down her anger at this newcomer's insult to her friends. She grudgingly admitted he was right. "I agree with you, but if they believed in ghosts, would they go looking for them? Wouldn't they be afraid of them? I think they are only curious about the lights, which I must admit are unusual. I've lived here forty years, and this is the first time I've heard of lights on the sides of the bluffs."

"Me, either." Effie crossed her arms over her Sunday gown and glared at him.

"Me, either." Evan imitated her, adding a definitive nod for good measure.

Libby disciplined a smile. The children had only lived in River's Edge two of their eight years.

Justin smiled, too, shaking his head. "I've lived here all my life, and I admit it's the first I've heard of such lights."

Copperfield pressed his lips together again. "I've tried to tell people the lights are likely nothing more than the reflection of lanterns from trains or carriages on the opposite bluffs, but people seem to prefer the ghost explanation."

Justin nodded. "Undoubtedly there is a reasonable explanation that does not include ghosts. Perhaps in viewing the lights, someone will discover the true explanation."

"Of course, they will," Libby agreed.

The lines in Copperfield's strictly disciplined face relaxed slightly, and Libby knew he was relieved to find someone who agreed with him.

Effie tucked her hand into Spencer's. Libby saw her eyes challenge Copperfield. "The captain is living on that old steamboat."

Copperfield looked at Spencer in surprise. "Is that true?"

Spencer met his gaze calmly and nodded.

"Have *you* seen any ghosts?"

"Not a single apparition."

Effie scowled up at Spencer. "What's an ap. . .ap. . ."

"Apparition," Copperfield snapped. "It means a ghost. If the captain lives out there and hasn't seen any, then there's no reason for you to believe in them, is there?"

"It's no reason not to." Effie tossed her curls. "Ghosts can be invisible if they want."

"Yes," Evan agreed.

"Children." Constance's voice held a warning note.

Ruddy color spread from Copperfield's shirt collar up over his face. Libby had the feeling he could barely suppress his rage. She was sure he wasn't accustomed to children standing up to him. She wondered whether the children really believed in ghosts or whether the idea simply intrigued them. She wouldn't be surprised if Effie took the stance she did only because she'd taken a disliking to Mr. Copperfield. Effie never had been one to meekly accept another's opinion, regardless of age.

Spencer rested a hand on Evan's shoulder and slid his arm around Effie's shoulders. Libby had the distinct impression he was warning Copperfield that the children had an ally, although she couldn't see any such warning in his face.

Copperfield turned away from Spencer and the children. Libby could see anger flickering in his eyes. "Would you attend the WCTU dinner with me later this week, Mrs. Ward?"

Libby almost sputtered in surprise, both at his abrupt change of subject and at the fact that two men had asked to escort her within minutes of each other and both in front of Spencer. It was a moment before she could make her thoughts and tongue work in unison. "Thank you, but I have an escort for that evening." She was glad it was true and that she needn't resort to Mr. Copperfield's company to discourage Spencer.

Surprise and displeasure crossed Copperfield's sharp features. He bowed slightly from the waist in a gesture Libby thought more a dismissal than a sign of respect. "Another time, perhaps."

"Yes," she murmured, not knowing what else to say. *Not if I can help it,* she added silently.

He walked stiffly away.

Libby avoided meeting Spencer's eyes, though she imagined his gaze burning into her.

Constance glanced at her over Maria Louise's shoulder. Laughter danced in her eyes, but she didn't embarrass Libby by remarking on the invitation.

Effie wasn't as reserved. "Thank goodness!" She plunked her hands on her barely there hips. "Who would want to go anywhere with Old Sour Lemons?"

"Effie!" Constance stared at her in horror.

"Effie!" Justin repeated, anger filling the one word.

A laugh burst from Libby's throat before she could stop it. The nickname was so appropriate.

Spencer was chuckling, too. Had he had the same initial reaction to the man, Libby wondered?

She caught Constance frowning at her and stifled her laughter. "We mustn't speak of others that way, Effie," she said, trying to get back in Constance's good graces.

"I don't see why not," Effie argued. "Old Sour Lemons doesn't speak nice about people, especially kids."

"We treat people as we would like them to treat us," Constance reminded her. "That isn't always the same as the way we think they deserve to be treated. Remember the Golden Rule?"

"Yes." Effie's shoulders lifted in an exaggerated sigh. "But I think people should treat me by the Golden Rule before I have to treat them by it."

"If everyone waited for others to be the first to be kind," Spencer said, "no one would live by the Golden Rule. That wouldn't be a very nice world to live in, would it?"

Effie thought a moment. "I guess not. But I still don't like to be nice to people who aren't nice to me first."

"Unfortunately, most of us feel just like you do, Effie." Spencer's gaze met Libby's. The sadness she saw in his eyes made her stomach feel hollow.

ten

The week that followed seemed unbearably long to Libby. Knowing Spencer was in River's Edge made it impossible to concentrate on her work. It was difficult to carry on conversations with her customers. Her mind drifted constantly to Spencer.

With every ring of the bells above the shop door, her heart leaped with the hope that Spencer had stopped to see her. Not once was it Spencer who set the bells tinkling.

Again and again she berated herself for wanting him to stop by. She was a bundle of conflicting emotions. Not only was she confused about Spencer, she was also upset with God and feeling guilty over her anger with Him.

"Why are You allowing me to go through this, Lord?" she cried one night in the privacy of her bedchamber. "Wasn't it enough that I saw Spencer marry someone else, that I must spend my life without him? Having him near again, knowing I can be his wife if I choose is too difficult! I've done as I believe You wish, refusing to marry him. Isn't that enough? Why must I live through the torture of having him near?"

After she'd sobbed until there were no more tears, she turned to the Bible, seeking comfort. She opened to Psalm 40. "I waited patiently for the Lord; and he inclined unto me, and heard my cry. He brought me up also out of an horrible pit, out of the miry clay, and set my foot upon a rock, and established my goings. And he hath put a new song in my mouth, even praise unto our God: many shall see it, and fear, and shall trust in the Lord."

A small wave of surprise rippled through her. These were the verses she'd clung to all those years ago when Spencer had eloped with Margaret. Back then, as tonight, she had thought the pain unendurable. Many times the pain had been so intense that she couldn't believe God could relieve it, ever, but she'd repeat the verses anyway and tell herself she believed God could take her out of that horrible place and give her a new song.

"And He did," she whispered, hugging the Bible to her chest. "I never forgot Spencer, but life became good again, filled with the love of friends, and family, and Joshua. God helped me before. He'll help me again."

She slid beneath the quilt, still clutching the book, and waited for sleep.

ச

Pastor Green's company at the Women's Christian Temperance Union pie dinner was more pleasant than she'd anticipated. He was easy to be around. Though politely attentive, he didn't fawn over her.

The most uncomfortable part of the evening was the knowing looks from the townswomen: the raised eyebrows, the sly grins, the whispered comments. *It would be bad enough if I wanted to be courted seriously by him,* she thought, *but it's worse knowing I'm only with him to discourage Spencer.*

The next day, townswomen again found their way to the millinery. Libby spent her time dodging questions about Pastor Green—she couldn't think of him as Daniel, as he'd requested—rather than selling hats.

"Such a nice man!"

"Yes," Libby would agree. "Did you notice the latest confection, the hat with the silk buttercups and lace-trimmed brim in the window? Just arrived from New York."

"You two looked so comfortable together."

"The pastor is an easy man to talk to," Libby would reply, keeping her tone brisk and businesslike. She'd pick up a hat from a display and hold it up for the woman to admire. "This style would look lovely with that fetching spring suit I saw you wearing at church Sunday."

The woman would glance obligingly at the hat, perhaps even try it on. "He seemed very attentive."

"He is a gentleman. This style is very becoming to you."

"He looks younger than the man you were with last week, but I'm not sure but what the other man looks more distinguished."

"They're both nice-looking men. Unfortunate that men haven't the opportunity to wear bonnets, isn't it? Amazing what the right style bonnet can do to emphasize a woman's beauty."

"Yes," the woman would agree absently. "It isn't often a widow your age has two such charming men courting her."

Knowing truth lay behind such comments didn't make them easier to swallow. Libby would grind her teeth to keep her replies bordering on polite. Often she'd turn her back on the customer, pretending to be busy with a display or selecting a hat and murmuring something unintelligible.

"I expect both would make responsible husbands." Eventually the comments always came around to marriage.

"I'm sure they would. However, as I'm not planning to marry either of them, I must continue to run the millinery. Did you notice this cute little item with the silk daisies?"

"Oh, I don't see just what I'm looking for today. I'll be back in a week or two and see what you have then that's new."

At six o'clock on the day after the pie dinner, Libby said good night to her assistant, Miss Silvernail. While she was preparing to close the shop, Ida joined her from the dress shop next door for their walk home.

"I didn't make a single sale today," Libby complained, checking over the special-order bonnet Miss Silvernail had completed trimming. "Even asking their opinion on the mysterious cliff lights didn't sway the so-called customers from their prey, meaning me. I felt like a rabbit with a flock of hawks after it."

"I don't think hawks hunt in flocks, dear." Ida picked up an ostrich feather from the trimmings table and pulled its softness across a palm. "Probably didn't make any sales because of your charming manner."

Libby set down the hat, frowning at Ida's tone. "Why do you say that?"

"When the women didn't get any news from you about

Pastor Green and that handsome captain, they came to my shop."

Libby groaned.

Ida chuckled. "Really, Libby, you should know better than to speak to Mrs. Keyes as you did."

Mrs. Keyes, the judge's wife. "Oh, Ida, you should have heard her, going on about 'poor old widow women' being like 'beggars who shouldn't be choosers' and how fortunate I was to have two men interested in me when there are younger, prettier, and wealthier widows available in town. It was disgusting."

"It's nothing we haven't heard before. To tell her 'at least the men I'm seeing have a choice with whom they'll have dinner.'" Ida clucked her tongue and shook the ostrich feather in Libby's face. "That was a bit much, all but saying her husband had to put up with her company."

Libby brushed aside the feather. "She deserved it, the old busybody."

"Yes, but you know better than to treat one of your best customers that way."

There was an all-gone feeling in Libby's stomach. Ida was right, of course, but she'd hoped Mrs. Keyes hadn't understood the insult. "How angry is she? Do you think she'll try to keep her friends from frequenting my shop?"

"Well, she's definitely insulted, and she is an influential woman in town."

Libby dropped her head into her hands.

"She's also a proud woman," Ida went on. "Once she's thought about it, I doubt she'll want friends to know what you said. I expect her anger would be mollified considerably if you offered her a good price on that darling peach French creation in your window. It will go perfectly with the dress she ordered from me this afternoon."

Libby lifted her jaw angrily. "That's the most expensive hat in my shop!"

"Angry words can be costly, can't they?"

Libby grabbed her cape from the wooden wall peg and threw it over her shoulders.

"It's hard to keep angry words inside, though," Ida went on in a lowered, softened voice, "when what people say is true, and we don't want to face it, isn't it?"

Libby stopped with her hand on the handle of the workroom door. Was that why she'd lashed out at Mrs. Keyes, because what she said was true? No. "What she said was cruel."

"So is the truth, sometimes. She was right. If I can't say it, who can? Neither of us will ever be young or pretty again. You're fortunate your niece introduces you to marriageable men and that the captain and Pastor Green are interested in you. I haven't had a decent man offer to escort me anywhere in years."

"There's more to a woman than youth and beauty."

"Men aren't inclined to look at the inner woman first."

"The decent men you mentioned will look at the inner woman eventually. Besides, having a man in one's life doesn't necessarily make life better."

Ida sighed deeply. "Easy for you to say, with two men courting you. You may not want to be married again, but I do. I like doing for a man. I don't expect passion." Ida's cheeks grew cherry red at her reference to the private side of marriage. "I only want a companion."

Libby bit back her immediate retort. Ida had never made it a secret she wanted to remarry. If that was her friend's desire, who was Libby to belittle it? She tried to smooth the ripples of anger from her voice. "I admit, I liked doing housewifely things for Joshua, but I don't know that I'd like doing them for just any man. I don't want to settle for a loveless marriage of convenience."

"I guess I'm not so picky. I've been widowed going on twelve years now. I don't want to grow old alone."

Libby slipped her arm through her friend's. "What are you talking about? Neither of us is going to grow old alone. We have each other, haven't we? If that's not fine companionship, I don't know what is."

eleven

"Yoo hoo! Captain Matthews!"

In the pilothouse where he was oiling the paneling, Spencer peered out the window. "What—" Who would be calling for him?

"Yoo hoo!"

On the shore stood Effie and Evan, waving their arms above their heads for all they were worth.

He leaned through the open window and waved. "Hello!"

Evan placed his hands about his mouth to form a megaphone. "We came to see you!"

"Wait for me there. I'll pick you up in the rowboat."

When they were all back on the steamboat, he showed them about. They'd already been over most of the boat on their "detectiving" visit, but this time Spencer explained different parts of the ship to them.

In the captain's quarters, Spencer scowled at his desk. He didn't remember leaving the papers in such disarray. He'd found them in the hidden panel in the wall behind the desk. Nothing there but old captain's logs and river charts. Still, uneasiness rippled through him, like a breeze causes ripples across otherwise calm water. On the first deck, he'd seen a lantern he hadn't recalled leaving out of place. In the dining hall, he'd found a bandanna that wasn't his.

Either strangers have been on board, or I'm getting addlepated in my old age. Had people from River's Edge been rummaging about the boat? It was surprising so little had been ransacked in the time the boat had been stranded. He knew of abandoned boats that had been stripped, their furnishings becoming parts of people's homes and businesses. He tried to shove away his uneasiness and gave his attention to the children.

The children's favorite spot was the pilothouse, at the very top of the steamboat. From there, they could look out in any direction.

Both pretended to work the wheel, which was taller than they were. "I bet you drove steamboats," Evan said confidently.

"Sometimes," Spencer admitted. "Most of the time, the pilot was at the wheel. The pilot is the most important man on a steamboat."

"Not more important than the captain," Effie said.

Spencer nodded. "Yes, he is. The pilot has to know all the turns and quirks of a river. If he doesn't, the boat can end up jammed on a bar like this one." He pointed out the front window. "See that tall staff at the very front of the boat?"

Evan nodded.

"That's called the jack staff. It's right in the middle of the boat's bow. The pilot uses it to guide the boat."

"Wow!"

He showed them some of the tools of the pilot's trade inside the pilothouse. They acted as though they'd been shown a toy chest.

"Can I blow the whistle?" Evan's brown eyes were large with hope.

"Me, too!" Effie jumped up and down.

Spencer grinned. All youngsters asked to blow the whistle on their first visit to a pilothouse. "All right, but only once each. Remember, whistles are the way steamboats talk to other people on the river and on shore. Don't want to confuse anyone."

After the great event, Evan turned to him. "What do you do out here all day, since you can't steer the boat anyplace?"

"Clean. Polish wood and glass and brass."

"Can we help?" Effie begged.

Spencer chuckled. "You want to clean an old boat?"

"It would be fun cleaning out here," Effie assured him.

"Yes," Evan agreed. "May we?"

"If your aunt and uncle agree to it, I'll be glad to have your help."

"Where do we start?"

"You can start by polishing the bell on the end of the texas."

Effie frowned. "Isn't Texas a state?"

"Sure is, but on a steamboat, the texas is the level below the pilothouse. The captain and officers have cabins in the texas." He grabbed some rags and polish. "Come on out, and we'll take a look at that bell."

The bell was huge, like all steamboat bells. Its brass was dulled from age and the elements. Spencer shook his head in disgust. He'd never allowed things to be so poorly maintained on his boats.

"Wow! This must be as big as the bell in the church steeple." Evan slid a palm over it in admiration.

Spencer showed them how to polish it. He was quite sure they would tire of helping him long before the bell was shining again. It was so nice out in the spring sunshine that he decided to help them instead of continuing his work in the pilothouse.

Evan's comments brought his thoughts back to the church and from there to the preacher. Not that his thoughts needed much encouragement to lead in that direction. He'd been picturing the preacher and Libby together all week.

His gut tightened at the thought. It was becoming an all-too-familiar sensation. He'd been so surprised Sunday to hear the preacher was escorting her to a function that he could have been knocked over by the proverbial feather.

How could I have been such a fool? he berated himself for the twentieth time since Sunday, while Effie and Evan chattered away as they worked. *Why didn't I suspect some other man would be trying to stake a claim on her? Her husband's been dead five years; she's long past the required mourning period when other men would refrain from courting her. The amazing thing isn't that other men are interested, but that a woman as fine as Libby hasn't remarried by now.*

Not just one man was interested. There were at least two. The preacher and Old Sour Lemons. He grinned. Couldn't quite imagine Libby with that last one. Looked like he hadn't a funny bone in his entire long, thin body.

But the preacher had him worried. He was just the kind of man Spencer would expect her to like: respectable, friendly, educated, and worst of all, he shared her faith.

He rubbed the bell furiously, wishing he could rub the picture of the smiling preacher and Libby out of his mind.

"Are you coming to church tomorrow, Captain?" Effie asked.

"Expect so, since tomorrow's Sunday."

"I like going to church. 'Specially since we got the new pastor."

Spencer's ears perked up. "New? When did he come?"

Effie shrugged. "A couple months ago."

"Did, uh, did he and your aunt Libby begin courting right away?" He was almost ashamed of himself, trying to get information about Libby from the children. Almost, but not quite. *All's fair in love and war,* he reminded himself.

"I'm not sure." Effie scrunched her eyebrows together as though trying to remember. "But the pastor came to dinner at our house one night when Libby was there."

The knot in Spencer's stomach tightened. "Is your aunt Constance happy about your aunt Libby and the pastor courting?" He remembered the smile Constance gave Libby on hearing the two would be attending that pie dinner Wednesday night.

Effie shrugged. "I don't know."

"Me, either," Evan said.

He'd struck out on that attempt. He'd almost gone to that pie dinner, but in the end, he hadn't had the courage to see Libby with another man. Hadn't talked to Libby all week, either. Trouble with a woman running a hat shop was that a man had so little excuse to stop into the store, and since she'd refused to allow him to court her, he felt he needed an excuse. Now if she ran a general store, or was a postmistress, or—

"We did hear Aunt Constance tell Uncle Justin something about Aunt Libby the other night when we were detecting," Effie interrupted his thoughts. "She said she wanted Aunt

Libby to find a man who loved her, because love was life's true treasure, or something like that." Effie stopped rubbing the bell and looked at him. "Do you think love's a treasure, Captain?"

He ruffled her hair and smiled at her. "I sure do, Effie. The greatest treasure."

"Even greater than the ghost captain's gold?" Evan asked.

"Even greater than that."

"I'd sure like to see those ghost lights." Effie stared up at the tall limestone bluffs that rose above the steamboat. "Too bad you haven't seen them, Captain."

"Told Copperfield I hadn't seen a ghost, not that I hadn't seen the lights."

Both children whirled to face him, wide-eyed, their mouths open. "Where were they?" Effie asked.

Spencer pointed out the window behind Effie. "On the side of those bluffs." He pointed out the back window. "And on the bluffs down there." Then he pointed toward the Wisconsin shore. "And over there."

"*All* those places?"

He almost laughed at the disappointment that hung on Effie's face. "All of them."

Effie and Evan exchanged frustrated looks.

This time Spencer did burst into laughter. "From your long faces, anyone would think you were planning to search for the gold yourselves."

Evan's gaze jerked to him. "Who, us?"

"Yes, you two." A chill ran along Spencer's nerves at Evan's guilty face. He laid a hand on one of each of their shoulders and bent over until his face was level with theirs. "I know you two are ace detectives, but climbing around those bluffs can be dangerous. I don't want you two doing that. Understand?"

Effie looked at her shoes. He felt her wriggling beneath his hand. "We understand."

He looked at Evan. "You, too?"

Evan nodded.

"Good." Relief loosened his stomach muscles.

The children glanced at each other and grinned. Bells tinkled ever so softly in Spencer's brain. He ignored the sound. He didn't believe the children would flat-out lie to him.

Effie looked at Spencer with wide-eyed innocence. "Are you going to look for the treasure? You could probably find it, since you live right here."

Spencer looked up at the cliffs. "Nope, I'm not going to look for that treasure." *The treasure I'm after is worth a whole lot more,* he thought, *just as Constance said.*

That morning, Libby could no longer face her nonbuying, too meddlesome customers. Besides, thoughts of Spencer made her too restless to work. She left the shop in Miss Silvernail's care and went to visit Constance.

The downstairs maid led her to the backyard, where Constance was watching one-year-old Maria Louise and their little white fluff of a dog roll about together in the new spring grass. Maria Louise's squeals of delight brought a smile to Libby.

Constance greeted her warmly, then asked the maid to prepare coffee and a plate of cookies. "I've missed seeing you the last couple days, but I didn't want to take Maria Louise out in the rain we've been having."

Libby assured her niece that she understood and sat beside her on the quilt Constance had spread over the grass. "I simply had to get away from the shop."

"What happened? You usually love your time there."

Libby explained about the customers.

Constance smiled gently. "I know it seems they are prying into your personal affairs, but most of them are interested because they care about you."

"I know." Libby sighed. *If Spencer were a Christian and I could welcome his attentions, perhaps I would enjoy their bantering questions,* she admitted to herself.

Constance gave Libby's hand a quick squeeze. "Now I'm going to be nosey. Tell me if you wish me to mind my own business. How was your evening with Pastor Green?" Her usually calm green eyes couldn't hide her curiosity.

"Pleasant."

"I'm glad. I do think he is a very nice man."

Thoughts darted about Libby's brain like a badminton shuttlecock. She was bursting to tell Constance the truth behind her acceptance of Pastor Green's invitation, but would she feel too vulnerable if Constance knew the truth?

"We enjoyed the captain's company at dinner last Sunday," Constance was saying. "He told us you knew each other when he was a young man."

Libby's heart started beating louder than a trolley car bell. *Did he tell Constance and Justin about the love we shared and how he married Margaret?* Before she could ask what he'd said, Maria Louise and Thunder tumbled onto the quilt.

Libby slipped her arms around Maria Louise's chubby waist and pulled her onto her lap. Maria Louise let out a squeal. "Good morning, Angel," Libby said in her ear.

The little girl stopped struggling, turned around, and gave Libby a hug. The immediate and complete acceptance in the chubby arms and soft cheek warmed Libby's heart. *What business have I to feel sorry for myself, when there's so much love in my life?*

The maid announced the coffee was ready, so Libby, Constance, and Maria Louise moved to the wide porch, which swept gracefully around three sides of the house. They relaxed in fan-backed white wicker chairs beside a round wicker table. Delicate chintz cups and saucers, matching coffeepot, cream pitcher, and sugar bowl, along with lace-edged tea napkins, lent an atmosphere of elegance to the simple repast.

Maria Louise sat on Constance's lap. It took a few minutes to convince her Thunder didn't need a chair of his own. Milk in a miniature mustache-style cup with two handles and a large sugar cookie kept Maria Louise busy while the women visited. Neighbors waved and called greetings as they strolled past, some pushing carriages, some with young children in tow.

Constance's conversation went back to the captain's visit. "He told the funniest tales of boyhood pranks, or perhaps I should say young manhood pranks, he and Justin's father pulled together. At least, I found them amusing. I expect neither of their mothers found them humorous."

A smile tugged at Libby's lips. "You're right. Spencer's mother always said she despaired of his becoming a worthwhile, respectable citizen. I recall one April Fools' Eve, Spencer and Justin's father changed the signs on the businesses after dark. When the owners went to their shops the next day, the barber found the shoemaker's three-foot-high wooden boot above his door, the barber's pole was in front of the church, the bakery was behind a real estate sign, a lawyer's finely scripted sign was over the saloon door, and the saloon's sign was over Mrs. Pickering's Dining Room and Tea Parlor. Mrs. Pickering was a vocal teetotaler."

They laughed together, picturing the mix-up on the frontier town's winding, dirt street.

Maria Louise joined in the laughter. A grin of tiny pearl teeth dimpled her cheeks. Both hands hit the table, palms down, causing the coffee cups to dance, the silver teaspoons tinkling a merry tune on the saucers. Constance and Libby grabbed the cups to steady them and laughed all the harder at Maria Louise's sheer enjoyment of life.

"What a wonderful sense of humor the captain must have," Constance said, when everything was orderly again.

"Yes, he always did."

"Did you know each other well?"

He didn't tell her, then, she thought. She took a sip of coffee, trying to decide how much to tell. *Why not the whole truth? I'm tired of spending energy trying to hide the past.* "We were in love." She lifted her chin and looked Constance in the eye.

Constance's expression softened. "I'm not surprised. His voice changes when he speaks of you."

"It does?"

"Yes."

Libby shifted on the seat cushion. "Having a former Pinkerton agent for a niece is downright uncomfortable at times. You see right through people."

Constance smiled. "Do you still care for him?"

Tears heated Libby's eyes. "Yes."

Maria Louise, tired of sitting with boring grown-ups, slid from her mother's lap, then stretched her arm out as far as it would go toward the sugar bowl. Constance gave her one sugar cube for Thunder, and the girl sat down beside the dog, happy once more.

Constance turned her attention back to Libby. "So that's why you weren't excited to spend an evening with Pastor Green."

Libby nodded. "One of the reasons."

"Why did you agree to his invitation at all, if you care for Spencer?"

"I wanted to discourage Spencer."

Haltingly, Libby started to explain. Soon the whole story tumbled out. "So you see, I can't marry him because he isn't a Christian."

"Perhaps he'll have a change of heart. I wasn't a Christian when I met Justin, either, remember."

"I'd forgotten."

"You mustn't give up on him, Libby."

"I know. I keep praying for him, but I can't marry him." Libby twisted her napkin. "Do you think I'm a foolish old woman, that I should settle for a good man I don't love?"

Constance's laugh danced out on the spring breeze. "Of course not!"

"Some people would."

"Some people are born old, with no sense of adventure or romance."

Libby smiled, more relaxed than she'd been since Spencer walked into her shop more than a week ago. "I was so worried you would think badly of me if I told you about Spencer. Instead, you've made me feel better."

"I could never think badly of you!"

"Sometimes, I feel guilty. I loved Joshua, but I've never forgotten Spencer. The thought has even crossed my mind that by allowing Spencer to come back into my life, God is punishing me for wondering about Spencer while I was married to Joshua."

"Oh, Libby!" Constance reached for Libby's hands. "Neither you nor the captain were unfaithful to your vows. I know you gave Joshua all the love that was in you while you were together."

Libby had to swallow twice before she could respond. "When Joshua asked me to marry him, I thought he was a wonderful gift from God. We were happy together, but the love I had for him was different than the love I have for Spencer."

"We never love two people exactly the same way. I'm sure you and Joshua were gifts to each other, for a season. That season is over. You mustn't feel guilty for caring for the captain or for anyone else."

"Learning how to live without Spencer all over again is hard."

Constance squeezed her hands. "I'll be praying for you and for Spencer, too."

Maria Louise threw herself against Constance's knees. "Up, Muvver, up!"

Constance drew her into her lap.

"Where are Effie and Evan?" Libby asked. If the twins were anywhere in the vicinity, she was sure she would have heard them by now, unless— She sat bolt upright. "They aren't playing detective again, are they?"

"Eavesdropping on us, you mean? No. They're off playing somewhere."

Libby leaned against the fan back, relieved. Sneaking up to hear adults' conversations was one of the twins' favorite ways of playing detective. It wouldn't do at all to have her confession about Spencer spread about town by those two little detectives-in-training.

twelve

Two weeks later, Spencer pounded a nail into unpainted lumber. The sweet smell of pine filled the room in the church basement.

"That should be it." He stood back to admire the bookcase. "What do you think, Daniel?"

Pastor Green, hands on his hips, black sleeves rolled up to his elbows, grinned. "It looks great. Thanks for the time you've given to make it. The Sunday school teachers and children will thank you, too. They haven't had anywhere to store their books and teaching supplies."

"Didn't do it by myself. We did it together."

Daniel ran a hand through his long, dark hair. "Nice of you to say so, but I know my talents as a carpenter will never put a true carpenter out of business. If it weren't for you, the bookcase would have remained nothing but a wish."

"Only the paint job is left. Have you bought the paint? Sooner we get started with it, the sooner we'll get done."

Before long, they were painting the shelves, Daniel starting at one end and Spencer from the other.

Spencer's thoughts, as usual, strayed to Libby while he worked. His plan hadn't been working out. He'd thought by becoming involved in the church, he'd see a lot of Libby. All he saw was her back during the weekly service. Instead of spending time with Libby, he was spending time with the other men in town at things like the men's Bible study.

The only times he saw Libby other than church were the times she dropped in at the Knights' while he was there. He stopped whenever he had a pretense. He was enjoying getting to know them. Unfortunately, whenever Libby found him at their home, she left as soon as possible.

Spencer decided since the church wasn't giving him more

time to spend with Libby, at least he could find out more about his competition. He had. To his dismay, the more time he spent with Daniel, the more he liked and admired him. The man was not only sincere in his faith, he was intelligent, compassionate, and got along easily with everyone. He knew Daniel was about the same age as himself and Libby, but Daniel had a youthful air about him, both in looks and manner.

Instead of encouraging himself by getting to know Daniel, Spencer was losing his faith in his own ability to win Libby's hand. *How could she help but fall in love with Daniel?* he asked silently, looking at the other man spreading white paint over the boards. *He believes in everything she believes in.*

Daniel looked over at him with a grin. "I do believe God sent you to us, Captain."

Spencer grunted. "I hardly look like the answer to anyone's prayers."

"Don't be so sure. Most of the church men are too busy to help with projects such as this."

"They're busy earning a living for their families. I'm retired."

Daniel laughed. "That doesn't mean you're sitting around whistling and whittling. You've told me how much work is involved in fixing up that steamboat. Besides helping with the bookcases, you've added a spark of life to the men's Bible study. When I came here, the group, though loyal, seemed to have fallen into a boring pattern. Your questions have livened things up, made the men think a bit about their faith again."

Spencer wondered what Daniel would think if he knew those questions weren't inspired by his desire to strengthen and understand his faith, but by his lack of faith and opposition to it. "I never could handle the idea of a God who's so weak He's threatened by a few questions from lowly humans." That, at least, was true.

"Me, either. I know we can't find the answers to all our questions. Some things we just have to trust God is handling, even when it looks to us like everything's a mess. Since He made us, He must realize we don't understand everything and that we'll have questions."

"Ever afraid your questions will pull you away from the faith, Daniel?"

"Now that's a scary question for a preacher to answer!" Daniel's eyes filled with laughter. "Pastors have been dismissed for lesser things than answering a question like that honestly."

Spencer shrugged. "Don't answer if you don't want to."

"When I've admitted to myself I have questions and have sought answers to them, I've usually grown stronger in my faith, not weaker. I do, however, have a list of things I sincerely hope the Lord will explain to me when we're all together for eternity."

Spencer laughed with him.

"As for being dismissed," Daniel went on, "I don't worry about things like that. I live as my conscience and, I believe, God's Word dictate. I've not yet been dismissed by a congregation. If such a thing happened, I'd trust God's hand was in even that."

Spencer's brush stopped. "You believe God is involved in everything that way?"

"I know there are some Christians who believe God's hand is in everything, as I do, and those who think He is only involved in the things we perceive as good. Most people wouldn't perceive being dismissed as a good thing. But what if I needed exactly that in my life in order to become open to a change I needed to make in my beliefs? Or what if the Lord had been trying to tell me it was time to move on, and I wasn't hearing Him or was resisting what He was trying to tell me? If I stayed, I might prevent just the man the congregation needed at that time from taking the position." He shrugged. "Maybe it doesn't work that way, but I think maybe it does."

"Sounds a lot like predestination."

"I don't think it's the same. God brings us to certain places in life, but we always have free choice in how to react in those situations. Our reactions determine where we go and how we grow next."

Spencer nodded. At least he agreed our choices determine our destinies.

"No, it's not predestination," Daniel was continuing, "so much as it is truly believing Romans 8:28: 'And we know that all things work together for good to them that love God, to them who are the called according to his purpose.' Too many of us give lip service to that verse, but don't believe it in our hearts."

Doesn't sound like it applies to people like me who don't love God, Spencer mused. *So Daniel believes God brought me here at this time. If that's true, I wonder why? Maybe so He could punish me for not believing in Him by letting me watch Libby marry this man who does believe in Him? If that's the way this God loves, I don't want anything to do with Him.*

Libby had said God had brought him to the steamboat at just the right moment to rescue the twins. If she and Daniel were right about things, was it possible the twins would have died if he hadn't come back to River's Edge?

A moment later, he snorted in disgust. What was he thinking? He didn't believe this silly God stuff. He was here for one reason only: to win Libby's heart back.

"Coming to the hymn-sing tomorrow evening?" Daniel's question broke into his thoughts. "It'll be held in the park behind the church. The members tell me there's usually a good turnout."

"I hadn't thought about it. Are you escorting Mrs. Ward to it?"

Daniel grinned. "Yes, I sure am."

Spencer's stomach felt tighter than a wet knot. "She's a wonderful woman."

"That she is."

Spencer cleared his throat. "Do you believe she's one of the reasons God brought you to River's Edge?"

Daniel met his gaze calmly. "Might be."

"How will you feel if she marries someone else? Will you trust that even in that, God is in control?"

Daniel's eyes narrowed slightly. "Why do you ask, friend? Are you interested in her yourself?"

Spencer hesitated. It was one thing to tell Libby his intentions. It was quite another to tell the man who appeared to have the advantage in her affections. His determination hardened. He was here to win Libby. He believed in speaking the truth. He nodded once, sharply. "I am."

Daniel studied him for a minute. "Thank you for your honesty." He walked over and held out his hand. "May God's will prevail."

Spencer shook his hand and nodded, trying to appear calm. His stomach turned over. If there was a God, Spencer didn't think it likely He was on Spencer's side. He wasn't at all sure he wanted God's will to prevail.

❧

The next morning, there was a guarded look in Daniel's eyes when he greeted Spencer at church. Spencer didn't blame him. He felt the same way.

He was pleasantly surprised when Effie and Evan begged him to sit with their family during the service. As Justin seconded their invitation, Spencer joined them.

His spirits soared when he found Libby was already waiting with Constance for the rest of the family. He tried to ignore the fact that she didn't look as pleased as he felt. In fact, she looked trapped.

Effie and Evan insisted on sitting one on either side of him. He'd have preferred sitting beside Libby, but as Libby sat on the other side of Effie—at Effie's insistence, bless her—he considered himself fortunate. He smiled broadly at her over Effie's head and was pleased when she responded with a smile of her own, though she immediately disciplined it and looked away.

When Daniel turned to face the congregation at the front of the church, his face was calm and welcoming. Spencer suspected he was the only one to catch Daniel's short pause when he caught sight of Spencer sitting with the Knight family. Daniel's gaze darted from Spencer to Libby and back again.

Spencer tried to play honorably and not grin, but he failed miserably. He couldn't resist smiling and feeling smug. Daniel needn't know Libby preferred that Spencer sit elsewhere.

He didn't envy Daniel, trying to keep his mind on his sermon while watching Spencer seated with the Knight family. He wouldn't want to be in his shoes.

Spencer was surprised to find his own attention caught by Daniel's sermon. He was speaking on the question Spencer had brought up to him the day before, whether God was involved in the ordering of everything in our lives. He listened carefully, wondering whether Daniel, who had answered his questions so respectfully yesterday, would speak of people who did not agree with his views disrespectfully today, when he had his image to uphold before the church members. His own respect for Daniel increased when the man didn't change his view in front of the church.

"Whether my beliefs on this are right or wrong," Daniel said, "I find that in believing God has a reason for everything He allows to happen in our lives, I am more open to asking what it is God has to teach me in each situation, rather than railing at Him for allowing it or making excuses for my own choices."

Following the sermon, Daniel announced the hymn-sing would be held that evening. Spencer was surprised when he next heard Daniel tell the congregation of Spencer's help in obtaining the wood and building the bookcases.

Spencer rubbed a palm over his beard. *This man makes it harder and harder to dislike him. I hate to admit it, but if he wins Libby's heart, she'll have a good man. Not that I intend to let that happen!*

After church, Effie clung to his hand. "Can we invite Aunt Libby out to see the steamboat, Captain? Evan and I have told her how we've been helping you. We want to show her what we've done."

Spencer glanced at Libby. Her face was a pretty rose color in embarrassment. "Mrs. Ward is always welcome on my steamboat."

Libby's color deepened.

Effie whirled around to face Libby. "You'll come, won't you?"

Say yes, Spencer urged silently, not taking his gaze from Libby's eyes. He could see the struggle she was going through inside. *Say yes.*

Finally, she nodded. "I'd love to see what you and Evan have been working on so hard."

"When?" Effie asked.

"How about right after church?" Spencer asked. "We can catch some fish and have a cookout."

"Or maybe I can pack a lunch," Libby said dryly.

Spencer laughed, happiness filling him. "Might not be a bad idea, just in case."

Daniel was friendly when he and Spencer shook hands at the church door, but he still had a guarded look in his eye. "It's not over yet," he succinctly reminded Spencer with a smile.

But things are looking up, Spencer thought, walking down the steps with a twin skipping on either side of him. *Things are definitely looking up.*

thirteen

Spencer had obtained a rope ladder, which hung over the side of the steamboat for easy boarding. At least, he found it easy boarding that way. The twins thought it an adventure.

Libby found it humiliating. The twins, who had been the first to scurry up the ladder from the rocking rowboat, stood on the lower deck, urging her upward. Spencer was right behind her, urging her forward, assuring her in his calm, low rumble that she could manage it just fine.

She wanted to push him off the ladder into the river.

She didn't dare. It would have meant hanging onto the ladder with only one hand. It was all she could do to lift her hands one at a time to move up each rung.

It wasn't like her to be frightened of anything, but she'd never climbed a ladder where the rungs sank beneath one's feet, over water, in an ankle-length skirt, with the man she loved but couldn't have right behind her. She tried to forget she didn't know how to swim.

I should never have agreed to come out here, she scolded herself, *but I couldn't turn the children down.*

Effie and Evan grabbed one of her arms when she reached the top, trying to drag her over the edge. With their help, she heaved herself onto the deck and sat, breathing hard from the unusual exertion and—she hated to admit it—from fear, her arm feeling like it had been pulled from the socket, while Spencer climbed aboard.

She was glad she'd worn her brown suit with the jet black lace today. Any woman who spent her day climbing ropes onto dirty steamboat decks couldn't afford to wear anything pastel and frilly!

"Have you ever been on a steamboat?" Effie asked her.

"Oh, my, yes. Back when Spen—the captain—and I were

your aunt Constance's age, everyone traveled by steamboat if they wanted to go any distance at all."

"What if a town wasn't built on a river?" Evan looked smug. "Then people couldn't go there on a steamboat."

"Most towns were built on rivers because it was easier to travel by river than to build roads."

"What about the railroad?" Effie asked.

"Weren't any railroads in this part of the country when River's Edge was built." Spencer put his hands on his hips and looked out over the river. "There weren't any railroads in Minnesota for a good ten years or so after the first settlers started River's Edge."

Effie and Evan frowned. They didn't look like they believed Spencer. "We came here from Chicago on a railroad." Effie looked as if she thought her comment would change Spencer's mind.

Spencer looked down at her. Libby wondered if it was sympathy she saw in his eyes when he answered. "I imagine you did. There aren't any rivers running from Chicago to River's Edge, more's the pity. Nothing compares with the romance of steamboat travel." He cleared his throat and rubbed his hand across his bearded chin. "Maybe we should show your aunt Libby around the boat before we go fishing." Spencer held out a hand to help her to her feet.

Once Libby was on her feet, Effie and Evan each reached for one of her hands. "Come on!"

Though Libby's heart warmed as always at their care for her, regret spread through her when she removed her hand from Spencer's to take the children's hands. She wondered, her breath coming more quickly at the thought, *Did our touch transport him back to when we were young and in love and all our dreams seemed possible?*

Spencer smiled at her over the children's heads. "Maybe we can find some places you haven't seen on a steamboat before. Let's show her the engine room first, twins."

The huge, wood-fired boilers didn't impress her nearly as much as the small galley, tucked into a tiny space near the boilers. "Imagine trying to prepare meals for an entire boat-load of people in this small space," she said, shaking her head.

"You have to see the dining hall." Effie led the way up the sweeping staircase to the next level. "That's the prettiest part of the whole ship."

"Boat," Evan reminded her forcefully, rolling his eyes.

Effie ignored him. "Hurry!" She ran down the deck, past the closed stateroom doors, toward the double doors leading to the dining hall.

Libby had seen many steamboats' dining halls, also called social halls or saloons, but she was curious to see this one. They were always elegantly decorated.

"Don't get your expectations up too high," Spencer spoke from beside her. "The prior owner kept up the parts that kept the *Jennie Lee* afloat and running, but he didn't spend any money taking care of the rest of her."

Effie and Evan each held one of the double doors. They playfully bowed when the captain and Libby entered.

"O-o-oh!" A sense of sadness and disappointment swept through Libby when she saw the room. It had obviously never been one of the more elegant ones on the river, but it had been lovely once. Spencer had been right; it hadn't been cared for.

She walked slowly down the middle of the long room, her steps noiseless on the once-thick carpet. She stopped beside a round walnut table with inlay, and ran an index finger across the top. The wood was scarred and water-stained. Gold-and-maroon-striped velvet on the side chair was threadbare and torn. The matching curtains at the window above the table were almost transparent in places.

Libby jumped slightly when Spencer spoke from behind her. She'd become so involved in the state of the room that she hadn't realized how close he was. "Do you think I'm a fool for wanting to refurbish her?"

"No." She shook her head but didn't turn to face him. "I understand that you would want to see her restored to her original elegance. Loving riverboating as you do, it must be painful to see a boat neglected this way. But it will take a lot of work."

"Yes, it will, but I have the time."

Effie climbed up on the side chair, her weight on her knees, her palms on the table. She grinned at Libby, her eyes wide with excitement. "See? Isn't it the prettiest room?"

"Yes, dear."

"Captain Matthews is going to let us help him wash the windows and polish the brass candlesticks and lights in here." Effie looked puffed with pride.

Libby looked at Spencer and lifted her eyebrows. "How nice of him."

Spencer shrugged his shoulders and spread his palms in a what-could-I-do look. "They offered to help. Wasn't that kind of them?"

"It was," she admitted.

"It's fun to work on the steamboat." Effie slipped off the chair and continued down the length of the room toward the stern.

The others followed. Libby saw that the floor-length, maroon velvet curtains that separated the men's from the women's areas were in better shape than the window drapes. She reached out to take their softness in her hand, remembering the days she'd traveled by steamboat. Then the women's area had been carefully guarded to protect women from the gambling and from the men who drank and smoked cigars in the men's saloon.

As they left the room, Evan tugged her toward another sweeping stairway. "You have to see the pilothouse. I think that's the best part."

When they entered the room, Evan went directly to the brass-bound wooden wheel. "This is where the pilot steers the boat."

Libby smiled at the obvious. "I see."

"Captain Matthews says the pilot is the one who steers the boat, not the captain," Evan elaborated, "except sometimes. I want to be a pilot when I grow up."

Effie gave an exaggerated sigh and rolled her eyes. "You can't be a pilot, Evan. We're going to be detectives, remember?"

Evan gripped the wheel tighter and stared out the window over the bow of the boat. "I'm going to be both."

Effie shook her head. "Boys will be boys."

Spencer coughed. Libby caught his laughing gaze and tried to swallow her own amusement.

Effie swung her arms wide. "The captain already did a lot of work in here. See how shiny all the brass things are?"

"Yes." Libby glanced at the brass lanterns and chandelier and the brass-ringed cords hanging from the ceiling. "Everything looks like new."

Spencer beamed.

Libby caught her hands behind her back. "I think perhaps this is Captain Matthews's favorite part of the boat, too, don't you, Effie?"

Effie grinned. "Yep."

Evan turned from the wheel and pointed to the cords, which were too high for him to reach. "Do you know what these do?"

"No. I've never been in a pilothouse before." Libby smiled at Evan. "Do you know?"

He nodded and stuck out his chest proudly. "The pilot pulls this one to stop the engines in an emergency. He pulls this one to call the captain. This one blows the whistle."

"Very impressive."

"Every steamboat's whistle sounds different," Evan explained importantly. He pointed to a long wooden tube sticking out of the floor near the wheel. "Do you know what this is?"

"I couldn't even guess."

"The pilot talks to the men in the engine room through it." Evan could barely reach his face to the top of the tube. "Hello, down there!" he called. He swung around. "Hey, Effie, why don't you go down in the engine room and see if you can hear me?"

"Okay!"

Spencer caught her shoulder as she turned to dash from the room. "Not so fast! Let's do that another time. We still have to catch our lunch, you know. I'm getting hungry, aren't you?"

Soon they were on the bottom deck. Spencer brought out some long bamboo poles. "Found these on board." He indicated a pail filled with mud. "Want to fetch out some nightcrawlers for me, Evan?"

"Sure!" Evan dropped to his knees beside the bucket and dug his hands into the mud without a moment's hesitation.

Libby cringed at the sight. She almost felt that mud beneath her fingernails.

Soon they each had a pole over the water. Libby was glad Evan had put the nightcrawler on her hook.

"It's so peaceful. No wonder you like living here." Libby looked out over the water. The river looked deceptively calm. She knew the currents in the middle were strong, in spite of only a few ripples on the surface. *Like the currents between me and Spencer,* she thought. *Always there under the surface, no matter how hard I try to deny them.*

Spencer smiled at her. "Remember the first time we went fishing together?"

Laughter bubbled up inside her at the memory. "It was my first time fishing *ever.* You made me put on my own worm and take the fish I caught off my hook."

"As I remember it, I *tried* to make you take the fish off, but you screamed bloody murder when you touched a fish for the first time."

Effie giggled. "Aunt Libby, you didn't!"

Evan joined in her laughter.

"Then she wanted me to throw 'the poor things,' as she called them, back in the water so they wouldn't die," he informed the twins.

"He expected me to prepare them for lunch," she defended herself. "I didn't know anything about filleting a fish."

The twins chuckled together.

"Your aunt became a good fisherwoman eventually."

Libby bowed her head in acceptance of the compliment.

"Do you still like to fish, Libby?"

It was a moment before she answered. "This is the first time I've been fishing since. . .since you moved away from River's Edge." She shrugged. "There were always other things that needed doing, and then, Joshua, my husband, didn't care to fish." *Besides, there were all those sweet, funny memories of the times we spent together fishing,* she thought.

"Tell us stories about when you were little," Effie urged them.

"How old were you when you came here?" Evan asked. "Were you about our age, eight?"

"Oh, I was much older than you, fourteen or fifteen."

They told the children what life had been like in the early settlement when they first came to River's Edge.

The children listened, fascinated, their interest broken only when pulling in the numerous fish they caught. They soon had enough for a meal. Spencer retrieved a cast-iron skillet and a coffeepot. "The stove in the galley is too large to prepare such a small meal. We'll cook over an open fire on shore, instead."

So Libby climbed back down the rope ladder, her heart in her mouth, certain she'd land in the Big Muddy instead of in the rowboat. Thanks to Spencer's strong hands at her waist as she climbed, that didn't happen.

On shore, Spencer led them to a small circle of rocks where Libby could see there had been numerous fires. Obviously he had cooked many meals here. The children helped him gather kindling. He stirred the ashes until the coals caught the kindling, then laid on larger pieces of wood. Soon the fire was going. While it burned down to cooking height, he filleted the fish. The children went off down the shore to play, with strict orders to stay out of the water and off anything floating in the water or hanging over it.

Libby spread her shawl on a fallen log near the fire and sat down, leaning her elbows on her knees and watching Spencer. "Thank you for being so wonderful with the children, Spencer."

He glanced up at her. "Nothing to thank me for. I like them."

"They like you, too."

"Effie reminds me of you—spunky."

For a couple minutes, silence stood between them. Libby noticed the sounds of the river lapping the shore, the breeze brushing the bushes along the base of the bluff behind them, birds and gulls talking as they looked for food.

"I used to wonder what it would be like, Libby, raising children with you, watching you love our children, watching them love you." Spencer's voice was low, unusually soft.

Her insides filled with a sweet aching. Tears sprang to her eyes. She pressed her lips together to keep the pain inside. *If I tell him I've wondered the same things about him, it will only encourage him to believe I might change my mind and allow him to court me.*

She watched him place the fish in the skillet, rake some coals to the edge of the fire, and set the skillet on a cast-iron spider over the coals. It gave her time to wipe the tears in her eyes discreetly away with her handkerchief and get her emotions slightly under control.

With the skillet safely over the coals, Spencer washed his hands in the river, dried them on his clean handkerchief, and came to sit beside her. His nearness caused even more turmoil inside her.

"Won't take long for the fish to fry. Suppose in a couple minutes we'll have to call for those mud-nosed tadpoles, as river men would call the twins." His smile told her he didn't think of the children in such uncomplimentary terms, yet she knew he didn't expect or want her to let the term go by without comment.

"What a terrible thing to call children, Spencer Matthews! Why, it almost sounds like cursing."

"Cursing? It's a term of endearment. I should know. On a riverboat, a man hears a lot of cursing. Lots of river sailors swear like you never heard before, even in the early days of River's Edge." He brushed sand from the knees of his pants. "Whenever I'd catch myself using such language, I'd remember you scolding me for using it when we were children."

His voice had dropped to that level that vibrated through

her so intimately. She wished he would quit doing that! It did disastrous things to her resolve.

"Remember how you used to do that, Libby?"

She nodded.

"You were always so good. Your goodness made me want to be a finer man."

"You were always a fine man, Spencer."

"Not so you'd notice. A fine man doesn't get drunk and elope with a woman he barely knows."

She hadn't an answer to that.

"I gave up drinking after that. Figured if I could mess my life and Margaret's up so bad after one episode, I didn't need it in my life."

"I'm glad." She was glad, too, that she'd been given the gift of finally knowing it. She looked down at her lap, twisting her handkerchief. "You messed up my life, too, that night."

He enveloped one of her hands in his own. "I'm sorry." He took a long breath, and she was surprised to hear the breath shake. "But if I hadn't married Margaret, you wouldn't have married me anyway, would you?"

It was true. She wouldn't have married him unless he became a Christian. Still, she wished things wouldn't have ended that way between them, so abruptly, so irrevocably.

"In all the years since I left River's Edge, I've tried to be the kind of man you'd respect. Margaret and I saw to it that the boys were raised in the church, and I attended services when I could. I've tried to live by the Golden Rule, loving my neighbors as myself."

"I believe you love goodness, Spencer, but that isn't enough. The Golden Rule ends with loving our neighbors. It starts with loving God with all our heart and soul and mind and strength."

His calloused, worn hands cradled hers. It was as though she could feel his love flowing from his gentle touch. She knew she should pull away from him, but it was so beautiful to feel this loved.

"How can I love God more than anything else when there's you in the world to love, Libby?"

With a small cry, she pulled back. "You mustn't love me more than God!"

Spencer gave a snort of disgust. "Truly, Libby, you can be the most mule-headed woman at times."

"Mule-headed!"

"Now, stop your sputtering. Yes, mule-headed. I admit, most of the time I like that about you. I wouldn't be interested in any weak female who doesn't know her own mind. But when you get to talking about God, there's no reasoning with you."

Libby opened her mouth to retort, but before she could, he continued.

"Why would I love a God who kept us apart? I've been angry at Him for thirty-five years, and I sure don't see any reason to stop now!"

Libby stared at him, one hand at her throat, stunned at his anger.

He glared back, his chest heaving.

Effie and Evan's laughter and the sound of their feet running along the shore broke into the stillness that lay between Libby and Spencer.

Spencer moved to the fire and bent over the skillet, turning the fish with a long stick. Libby opened the wicker picnic basket she'd brought and removed plates and silver with shaking hands. They weren't shaking anywhere near as fast as her heart.

Libby smiled and nodded as Effie chattered away, displaying a round, river-polished stone, but all the while, Libby's mind was reliving the words between her and Spencer.

Suddenly, a thought occurred to her. *How can he be angry with You if he doesn't believe You exist, Lord?* In the midst of her confusion and anguish, a sliver of hope poked through. *Is it a start, a place faith can take root and grow, or am I grasping at straws? Don't give up on him, please, please don't give up on him!*

fourteen

At least the children don't seem to notice the tension between Spencer and me, Libby thought, watching them trailing their hands in the water over the sides of the rowboat on the way back to River's Edge.

Effie and Evan were chattering away about their plans for future picnics and walks along the bluffs, apparently not realizing the adults' lack of response.

Seated in the bow, Libby had to look past Spencer, who was rowing, to see the children. She was thankful his back was to her. *I couldn't bear to look into his stony face all the way back.*

"Captain, what's it like to be old?" Evan asked, still watching his fingertips forming a "V" in the water.

Spencer snorted. "Old?"

Libby pressed her fingers to her lips.

"Humph. Guess I do look old to you," Spencer responded.

"Of course," Effie agreed. "Don't *you* think you look old?"

Libby's sudden coughing spasm caused her to almost miss his reply.

"Depends on who I'm comparing myself to." His oars dug into the river again. "Getting older means my mind and heart become like a scrapbook of memories. The older I get, the more memories I have; memories of places I've seen, things I've done, and the best memories, of people I've known and loved."

Libby's heart swelled with love for him. What a lovely way to answer a child. What a lovely way to look at growing old.

Effie smiled mischievously. "Are we in your scrapbook?"

"You sure are. I hope I'm in yours and Evan's, even when you're as old as I am."

"You will be," Effie assured him.

Evan nodded decisively. "Absolutely."

And in mine, always, Libby added silently.

They passed another rowboat, headed in the opposite direction. The woman in it waved cheerfully.

Libby waved back, surprised to see her. She didn't recall that family spending much time on the river.

For that matter, there seemed an inordinately large number of rowboats out. "Are there always this many people on the river?"

Spencer grunted. "More every evening. Some are fishermen, but I suspect most are out to see the lights. A number of people have stopped to ask if they can watch from the *Jennie Lee.* I said yes to the first few but started turning them away as the numbers grew."

"I had no idea people's interest had developed into. . .this."

"People come out by land, too, as Old Sour Lemons said. They'll build a town out here pretty soon," he joked.

At the landing, a wiry young man with an unkempt, scraggly beard met their boat. "Howdy, Captain." He caught the rope Spencer tossed to him and secured the boat to a dock pillar.

"Hello, Adams."

"I'll watch out for your boat while you're in town. With all the folks headin' out to see the lights, almost have to post armed guards out here."

"Thanks."

"I hear you're working on that old steamboat. I was wonderin' if you could use some help?"

"I hadn't considered hiring anyone. I've been enjoying doing the work myself, just idling time away."

Libby thought Spencer looked rather impatient with the younger man.

"P'rhaps you'd think on it?"

"Sure."

Libby looked back over her shoulder at the man as they left the landing. "Do you know him, Spencer?"

"Met him when I rented a rowboat. Name's Adams. He's waitin' for the steamboat he works on to arrive upriver."

Spencer walked them to the Knight house, then insisted on

walking Libby home. She wished he hadn't. It was an uncomfortable walk. *The air is so thick with tension, we could eat it like oatmeal if we had spoons,* she thought.

When they reached Libby's house, she was surprised to see Pastor Green having coffee with Ida on the front porch. She stopped short at the gate that opened to the lane leading to the house and clapped a hand to her throat. Dismay spiraled down through her. "Oh, my!"

Spencer grasped her elbow, bending his head toward her. "What? What's the matter?" His voice was filled with concern.

"N–nothing."

Ida spotted them and waved. "Hello!"

Pastor Green grinned and waved, balancing a cup and saucer in one hand.

Libby tried to smile and returned their greetings.

Spencer stiffened. "Guess I should have realized the problem right off. It's Daniel, isn't it? You're upset he's here with your friend."

"Yes. No. I mean. . ." It was so embarrassing to admit! She went through the gate, turning around to face him as she closed it. Her hands gripping two of the boards, she leaned forward and whispered, "I'm late. I forgot that he is escorting me to the hymn-sing. What must he think?"

Without waiting for an answer, she turned and hurried up the walk.

Pastor Green had risen and started across the porch. With her attention on him, Libby was shocked to hear Spencer's voice behind her.

"Evening, Daniel. Enjoyed your sermon this morning."

Libby whirled. "I thought you'd left." Immediately she wished she could swallow the words. Pastor Green must think her extremely rude.

Spencer ignored her and held out his hand to Daniel, grinning.

Daniel shook it. "Captain."

Why is he looking at Spencer so strangely? Libby wondered. Usually the pastor was engaging, trying to put others at ease, almost always smiling.

Ida bustled forward. "I was beginning to think you'd fallen in the river, and instead of attending a hymn-sing, we'd be dragging the bottom for you."

Libby scrunched up her nose in distaste. "Pleasant thought." She turned to Pastor Green. "I am so sorry. I'm afraid I lost track of time. We had a fish fry, and then we had to take the children home, and—"

"It's all right. I'm sure the people have started without us." He gave her his smile, trying to ease her discomfort, as usual. "Not only do they not need me to praise the Lord in song, they are probably glad to enjoy some hymns without my tone-deaf voice."

Ida laughed as though it were the only joke she'd heard in her lifetime.

Libby smiled politely.

"You'll want to freshen up a bit, I believe, before leaving for the hymn-sing." Ida made shooing motions with her plump fingers. "Don't worry about the menfolks. I'll keep them company until you get back." She smiled widely at the pastor and Spencer. "More coffee?"

Libby made her way slowly to the door, looking back over her shoulder at the group. Discomfort niggled at her. *Why didn't Spencer leave? Surely I made it clear that I'm attending the hymn-sing with Pastor Green.*

Still, she couldn't help smiling as she hurried up the stairs to her room. Ida, she knew, was enjoying herself immensely entertaining the men.

Libby's uneasiness over Spencer's presence followed her to the hymn-sing. When she'd returned to the porch after freshening up, Ida had cheerfully informed her that she and Spencer would be accompanying Libby and the pastor.

Before they reached the park, they discovered that Pastor Green had been right about the group beginning without them. They could hear the wonderful words of "Amazing Grace" floating through the early night air blocks away. When they arrived, they saw the choir director was leading the group.

Pastor Green led Libby, Spencer, and Ida to the front. Libby felt as if all eyes were upon them. *I dread the questions and comments this will raise from tomorrow's customers! Maybe I should offer to answer one question for every hat that is purchased. That should raise my sales.*

Seeing them arrive, the director motioned Pastor Green to the front. He apologized easily without explanation for being late, said he hoped everyone would enjoy the evening, and gave the direction back to the director. Then he rejoined Libby.

Twilight had given way to darkness. Gas streetlights, torches, and handheld lanterns lent light to the singers and cast the trees about the park into deeper shadow. It was a nice atmosphere, a nice change of place in which to worship, Libby decided.

Libby could remember when the townspeople had planted the trees. There had been hardly any trees in the town when her family moved here.

Her memory wandered. She knew if she looked around the group, she'd know almost every face. Many of them were old settlers, like herself. Most of the rest were their children or grandchildren. She knew the stories of most of their lives, knew the businesses they'd started, the dreams that had thrived, the ones that hadn't, had seen young love grow deeper in marriages, had seen hearts broken, like her own.

Together, these people had built this town, made it what it was today. She was part of them, and they were part of her. It was special, feeling she belonged to something larger than herself. In a way, as much as she disliked the interest the townspeople were showing in her escorts, she felt she was betraying her friends by allowing the pastor to escort her, as if her very behavior was a falsehood. *I must tell him I can't see him anymore,* she decided.

Her decision made, she turned her attention back to the hymns. She did love singing, especially hymns. She could tell the pastor did, also, though the comments he'd made about his voice back at the house weren't much of an exaggeration.

She saw Constance and her family across the crowd and

smiled at her. As her gaze swept the crowd, it met Mr. Copper-field's. His scowl showed he wasn't pleased she'd attended with Pastor Green instead of himself. Libby was glad she wasn't attending such a happy event with such an unhappy man.

Spencer stood on the other side of Ida, but Libby could hear his voice booming out on the familiar verse, "Oh, how I love Jesus!" Her heart crimped at the sound. *If only it were true!* she cried silently.

Why had he come tonight? She hoped he hadn't asked Ida to accompany him, at least not in a manner that would indicate he intended the evening to be more than friends spending time together. She didn't for a moment believe he was interested in Ida, and she didn't want her friend's feelings hurt.

She was sure he hadn't come because he loved to praise the Lord; not after the conversation they'd had on the beach.

It was becoming increasingly difficult to have him near. She wasn't sure how much longer she could bear seeing him and knowing they couldn't be together. Perhaps eventually his love for her would dissolve when he realized she would not change her mind, perhaps realize for himself that their love couldn't survive if they didn't share their faith. She didn't want that to happen either—for their love to actually die.

She glanced at him over Ida's head. How often in church as a young woman and again during the last few weeks she had imagined them standing together in church, worshipping the Lord from their hearts. If only it could be true. If only—

Her heart continued the prayer it had started so many years before.

❧

Spencer bent into the movement of the oars. The current had been getting stronger the last few days. The river was slowly rising, too. Both were to be expected. It was normal for the river to crest the middle of May in this part of the country, give or take a week. Unless he was mistaken, the *Jennie Lee* would be ready to float off the sandbar in a week, maybe a week and a half.

His mind drifted back to Libby, as it always did, as faithfully as a compass needle pointed north. It had been fun at the hymn-sing tonight, but he would have enjoyed it more as Libby's escort.

He grinned into the night. It had done his heart good to see the uncertainty in the pastor's eyes when he'd come up the walk with Libby, especially after the beating that heart had taken from Libby earlier in the day.

He looked up at the stars. "Why do I keep handing my heart over to her to slice up? You'd think I'd learn. She does it every time. But I know she loves me, I *know* it. I can see it in her face. Everything about her betrays her love, but she won't speak it. Instead she keeps trying to push me away. I don't understand. How can a love for You be so strong she won't go against her beliefs and marry me?"

He snorted. There he went again, talking to that God he didn't believe in.

It was beautiful out on the river tonight, with the moonlight shining off the limestone cliffs. He rounded the bend and saw the lights of the *Jennie Lee.* He didn't light the entire boat, but he always made sure there were enough lights burning that other boats would see her. Not only darkness was a threat; mornings on the river were often foggy. The *Jennie Lee* was grounded out of the usual travel lanes, but still, one couldn't be too careful. He wondered for the fiftieth time what the pilot had been thinking to be sailing so far out of the usual steamboat path when the *Jennie Lee* hit the bar.

He hoped the spring crest would free the *Jennie Lee* before some large debris carried by the high water hit her. At least there shouldn't be any danger from log floats. Back when he and Libby had been courting, it was common to pile the huge cut pines in the forests up north on the frozen river during the winter and float them down to the sawmills at places like St. Anthony and River's Edge. Why, he could remember when a man could walk across the Mississippi hereabouts on logs.

His glance slid along the bluffs on either side of the river. No mysterious lights in sight. Of course, on such a brightly lit night as this, lights might not be necessary.

The light watchers had apparently given up for the night. He hadn't seen many boats out on his way home.

He was pretty well convinced that Effie and Evan were at least partially right in their beliefs about those lights. Someone was searching for something, and the dead captain's rumored treasure was as likely a goal as anything. There were plenty of tales of hidden and lost treasure along the length of the Mississippi. But he hadn't a doubt the searchers were made of flesh and blood. He'd never heard of a lost treasure tale that didn't bring out people looking for an easy way to wealth. He shook his head at the thought of it. It didn't sound like the easy way to him.

Once on board, he started around the lower deck, taking his usual check of the boat before retiring. He grinned, laughing at himself. "Old habits die hard, I guess."

Entering his cabin at last, he stretched, looking forward to the comfort of bed. His foot struck something, and he stumbled, hearing a crash.

In the light of the moon coming through the open door, he saw an unlit tin lantern lying on its side, a pane of glass broken. The hair on his neck rose to attention, sending a prickly sensation along his nerves. Slowly, he knelt down and righted the lantern. It wasn't his. He hadn't set any lanterns inside the door. He didn't even have any tin lanterns on board; they were all brass.

Was whoever left it still on board? His mind raced through the path he'd just taken through the boat. He'd thought he'd looked at everything, into every room, but he knew there were hundreds of places a person could have hidden.

Why did they leave their lantern behind? he wondered. Maybe they'd forgotten it because they hadn't needed it on deck in the moonlight. *What were they looking for?* That question wasn't so easily answered.

Well, sleep is out of the question until I convince myself I'm alone on board. He glanced about his quarters, looking for something easy to carry that was heavy enough to serve as a weapon in case he needed one for self-defense. He settled on an old spyglass.

Keeping as much as possible to the shadows, he made his way along the texas, looking into each stateroom. Nothing.

He'd checked the pilothouse last thing before entering his own quarters on his first check, so ruled out the need to look there again. Taking each step as quietly as he could, he made his way down the steps to the next deck, his heart in his throat. It would be easy for a man to hide beneath the stairs and attack him before he even knew he was there.

Quit imagining things! one part of his brain ordered. *Pretty soon you'll have yourself believing in Effie and Evan's ghost.*

It's not imagination, it's caution, another part of his brain assured him.

Neither voice stilled the fear rippling through him.

He was gripping his spyglass so tightly the muscles in his hand were cramping. He changed hands, flexing the fingers in his right hand.

He took a deep breath when he reached the bottom of the stairway. Swung his head quickly to the left, then the right, but saw no one leaping to attack him. His breath whooshed out in relief.

For a moment, he looked around uncertainly. Which way should he go first? To the left or right? Maybe the wisest move would be to see whether there were any boats alongside the *Jennie Lee*. There hadn't been when he'd returned, at least on the side nearest shore, where he'd tied the boat at the bottom of the rope ladder.

His senses were heightened. His ears hurt from trying to hear anything unusual. The sound of the river lapping against the boat's hull was louder than normal. Every ordinary creak of the boat made him want to jump.

He took a long look up the deck, studying each shadow, waiting to see if any of the shadows moved. Tightening his hold on the spyglass, he moved quickly to the railing and looked over. Nothing but water.

He glanced again in each direction. Behind him. Nothing stirred.

Swallowing the lump of fear in his throat, he began searching the passenger deck.

By the time he'd completed the search, poking his head into every nook and cranny he could think of that could possibly hide a man, his chest hurt from the many times he'd held his breath. He'd found nothing, but he wasn't reassured by his search. It had taken over an hour. It would be easy for a person, or more than one, to have slipped back to an area he'd already searched.

So what should I do? Leave my own home? It was tempting to climb into his rowboat and leave, he had to admit, but he wasn't going to give into his fears that easily.

What were they looking for? He still didn't know the answer to that question. It was well known in town now that he lived on the boat. It was probably just a common thief who left the lantern.

Or Effie and Evan's treasure hunter.

More likely, it was left by some of the light watchers. A lot of them had asked to come aboard the *Jennie Lee,* where they could watch in comfort, as he'd told Libby. Matter of fact, more than once he'd found people who had boarded in order to find him and ask permission to stay. He wouldn't be at all surprised if some of them had taken advantage of his time in town to use the boat.

The possibility eased his fears enough that he headed up to the texas and his quarters, but it was almost dawn before he fell into a fitful sleep. It was the first time since he'd decided to return to River's Edge that he fell asleep with something other than Libby on his mind.

fifteen

" 'Bye, Captain!" Effie waved, starting off for the path that led to the top of the bluff.

" 'Bye, Captain! Thanks for everything. We had a great time." Evan waved and headed down the narrow, barely visible path through the scrubby growth at the bottom of the bluff. Thunder, their neighbor's little white fluff of a dog, trotted at his heels.

"Good-bye!" Spencer stood on the narrow beach, watching them, frowning, until they were out of sight, hidden by the thick underbrush between the break in the bluffs.

Worry crawled through his stomach. Should he have let them go alone? Why not? Hadn't Constance and Justin said they might walk home alone? The path, though overgrown here, was well known to the townspeople and well used. It led to a dirt road by which people often came out to picnic. They should be safe. "Something just doesn't feel right."

Quickly, he checked the rowboat to make sure it was pulled up far enough onto shore and hauled out the anchor and wound the anchor rope around a tree, to be doubly sure the boat wouldn't float off. Then he turned and started toward the path.

"Captain Matthews! Hello!"

He turned toward the river and voice in surprise. He wasn't expecting anyone.

A young man waved from a rowboat out near the *Jennie Lee*. "Hello, Captain!"

Spencer squinted, trying to make out the face. "Why, it's Adams."

The man was obviously heading toward shore. Spencer waited impatiently. He looked over his shoulder toward the path, eager to join the children.

Adams nosed the bow of his boat up to shore and jumped out into the shallow water, paying no mind that the water went over the ankles of his boots. Spencer grasped the nose of the boat and hauled it further onto shore.

"Thanks." Adams's skinny fingers settled on his lean hips, and he looked toward the bluffs, his constant smile in place. "Nice. Must be like ownin' your own piece of river, livin' on a river queen and havin' a piece of shore to rest on whenever you've a mind to."

"I like it," Spencer admitted, cautiously, "even though my river queen's a bit shabby."

"That's what I'm here 'bout. Wondered if you'd thought any 'bout my offer ta help out."

Spencer rubbed the back of his neck. "Have to admit, I haven't."

Adams shrugged his shoulders up about his ears in a manner that reminded Spencer of a turtle trying to decide whether to hide or stick its neck out. "Is that a no?"

"No. It meant exactly what I said. I haven't thought about it."

Adams nodded, his head bouncing. "Well, guess that's good. You see, it's like this. I got to thinkin', maybe if I helped you out with the boat, you'd let me stay on board." He shook his head, still grinning. "You know how it is. Stay on land too long, I begin to feel like my bones clank."

Spencer's mouth tugged in a smile. "Yes, I do know."

"I'm a hard worker. I'll be glad ta help you just for a bed."

Spencer hadn't any doubt the man was a willing worker. He'd seen him about the docks often enough, and he'd never appeared to be shirking or lollygagging. "I'm sure your help would be worth more than a bed."

Adams gave a sharp little nod. "Thank ya."

Spencer studied the wiry man's eyes. *No reason not to hire him, I guess. Could sure use the help.* "All right. I'll show you what I'd like done. If you still want to stay on after that, we'll talk about pay."

Adams's grin widened. "Thank ya. That sounds good ta me."

Spencer had the absurd impression that Adams's grin was

as permanent as a rag doll's. He turned for a last look at the path the children had taken. They had quite a head start on him. He'd probably never catch up to them now. Still, he wavered for a moment. Should he head after them?

"Captain?"

It's likely too late. I'm being a paranoid old man. What harm could come to them along the path on the road to town? He swung around. "Let's head out to the *Jennie Lee*."

An hour later, he and Adams had worked out an agreement, and Adams had started back to River's Edge to retrieve his few belongings. Spencer looked out the pilothouse window toward the bluffs, unease drifting into his chest like smoke, definitely there, but intangible, unable to be grasped. *Why can't I shake this silly fear?*

The limestone bluffs stared back at him, mute.

The lights had danced along those bluffs again last night. The children had stayed overnight with him on the boat. They'd been fascinated by the lights. It had rained the last three days, but the storm had moved off just in time for Effie and Evan's visit. The sky last night had been clear and starlit.

Before the lights came out, the children had asked him to tell them stories of other hidden and lost treasure along the Mississippi. He'd enjoyed the telling of them, embellishing them as he had when his own children were small. Between his stories and the lights, he'd thought the children would never calm down enough to sleep.

"Should have known better. My own boys would have reacted the same way when they were Effie and Evan's age."

He'd seen the lights too many times not to have wondered about them. *Are they from lanterns carried by people looking for the rumored treasure? Maybe those who are carrying the lanterns are trying to attract attention from the areas where they are concentrating their search.*

Of course the lights were carried by humans. No doubt in his mind about that. But who?

River's Edge was a small town. Surely if the treasure hunters were residents, someone would notice them missing every night, or tracking limestone around on their boots, or sleeping all day because they'd been working all night.

"Could be newcomers or strangers in town," he mused. "Maybe bachelors, men whose actions no one would notice."

That man who had asked Libby to the pie dinner, the one she'd turned down, the one with the crimped face, was a newcomer and a bachelor. "Old Sour Lemons," he remembered, grinning. "Almost wish he *was* courting Libby. Sure would have a lot more faith in my ability to win her away from him than from Daniel."

Daniel. Another newcomer and unmarried. Spencer considered the possibility. Shook his head. He couldn't imagine Daniel clandestinely climbing the bluffs looking for treasure.

Of course, the river and railroad brought strangers to town every day. The treasure hunters could be one of a hundred men or more, he guessed. He snorted. "Why waste my time on it? Treasure hunters aren't thieves. If they want to climb about on cliffs at night, who am I to say they shouldn't?"

A movement toward the bottom of the bluff near where the path disappeared into the underbrush caught his eye. He scowled, trying to make out the form that was emerging. "What! Surely not!"

He grabbed the spyglass. Peered through it. It was. "Libby! What's she doing here?"

His heart took off like a pheasant routed from hiding during hunting season. She was actually coming to him, without the children prodding or any coercion, for the first time since he came to River's Edge.

He raced out of the pilothouse and down to the texas. Did he dare let himself hope she came to let him know she cared?

He threw himself against the railing. "Libby! Stay there. I'll take the boat and meet you!"

Spencer made the trip from the texas to the rowboat in record time. He fumbled with the knot securing the rowboat to the paddle wheeler, wasting precious minutes with it. When he arrived at shore, after much too much time according to his heart's calculations, he slipped the boat along the exposed roots of a tree, where he could jump out quickly without getting soaked.

Libby stood silently, watching him tie the boat to the tree. Spencer thought she looked great in her navy blue walking suit and prim straw hat with matching navy blue ribbon about the crown.

He was beside her in a few strides, feeling as though his grin couldn't grow any wider. He reached for her hands. "Libby, what are you doing here?"

"I came for the children. Are they on the boat?"

His chest felt like a band had been bound around it. "They left for home over an hour ago. Constance and Justin had said they might walk home. They took the path up the bluff to meet the road into town. You must have come by the same path. Didn't you meet them?"

She shook her head. Her eyes were wide with fear. Her hands clutched his. "Constance decided she would feel better if someone met the children and took them home. She and Justin couldn't come, so they asked if I would. I took the carriage as far as possible and the path the rest of the way." She glanced down at her feet, and Spencer's gaze followed hers. Limestone mud from the bluff path caked her high, buttoned boots and colored the hem of her skirt.

Her gaze slid back up to meet his. "Where can they be?" Her voice cracked on the whisper.

He couldn't bear to look into the terror in her eyes. His arms slipped around her. He pressed her cheek against his shoulder and touched his lips to her hair. "Shhh, dearest. It will be all right. We'll find them."

He squeezed her tightly, trying to will strength and hope into her, then took one of her hands in his. "Come on. We'll follow the path. They must have turned off to explore somewhere. You know Effie and Evan. If an adventure calls, they'll answer."

She followed along, one hand trying to hold her skirt back from twigs and sticky weeds. Her quick steps kept up with his long strides. "You. . .you don't think they've gone looking for the dead captain's hidden gold, do you?"

It was exactly what he thought. Wished he didn't. "I guess we'll find out."

The path was still almost level with the ground about it and had only begun to rise, when he began to call. "Effie! Evan!"

Libby joined in. "Effie! Evan! Where are you?"

Soon the path began to climb. It had developed over the years by people following the easiest way down to the river from the top of the bluffs, so it was not too narrow or difficult to walk in most places. Spencer soon realized why Libby's shoes were so mud-covered. The rains had left the path soaked and slippery. The mud almost oozed about his shoes, clutching at each of his steps. Even so, he could see in the mud where Libby had slipped and slid along the steeper parts.

"Effie! Evan!"

He or Libby repeated the call every few moments. He turned to smile reassuringly at her over his shoulder and squeeze the hand he still held. Her fingers were clutched about his like a vise wrapped in soft cloth. She was holding up well.

"Effie! Evan!"

"Yip! Yip! Yip!"

He stopped. Listened so hard it felt like his ears were growing. Had he imagined it? "Did you hear that?"

"Hear what?" Libby asked.

Imagination, or wishful thinking that he'd heard Thunder's high yip. He tried to push away his disappointment and kept walking. "Effie! Evan!"

"Yip! Yip! Yip!"

"I *did* hear it!" He stopped so suddenly that Libby walked right into him. He felt her clutching his coat to keep from slipping. "Did you hear it that time?"

She shook her head.

"I thought I heard Thunder."

He watched her, standing still as stone, listening. Nothing. "Effie! Evan!"

"Yip! Yip! Yip!"

Libby's eyes widened. Joy flooded them. "I heard him!"

"They can't be too far. Thunder wouldn't have left them." They started up the path again, faster, calling, then listening. A couple yards farther along, another sound joined Thunder's barking, a sound that sent fear pumping through Spencer's veins.

"Help!"

Let it be my imagination, he prayed.

"Effie! Evan!" Libby called.

"Shhh!" Spencer turned around and clasped his hand firmly but gently over her mouth. *She didn't hear it,* he realized. "Listen."

He saw the question in her eyes and looked away. He didn't want to see the fear in her eyes when she heard. Made himself look back. He wanted to be there for her, needed to be there for her.

"Yip! Yip! Yip!"

"Help! Help!"

Her eyes widened and filled with fright. He slid his hand from her mouth. "Effie?"

He nodded.

"O-o-oh!"

"We're right where we should be. The awful thing would be if we weren't where we could hear them."

She took a trembling breath. Nodded.

Spencer knew what he said was true, but he wished the words brought him more relief from fear. Why didn't they hear Evan calling? "Come on, let's find them." He squeezed her hand.

Her smile quivered.

His heart ached for her. Was she, too, silently wondering about Evan? He made a megaphone of his hands. "Effie! We're coming! Keep calling!"

She did. The calls changed from "Help" to "Over here!"

After what seemed several lifetimes, Spencer spotted a place where someone had slid off the path into the scrubby woods. He pointed out the signs in the mud to Libby and led the way into the trees.

The branches were thick and low. They had to push their way through them. Spencer was careful not to let any whip back and hit Libby. He thought he spotted signs others had passed that way; broken branches, the fallen leaves of years pushed slightly to one side here and there, as if a step had slid in them. He continued calling as they went and breathed easier as Effie's voice grew louder.

"Up here! Look up!"

They did. At least twenty feet above them, just at the height where the treetops began to hide the limestone cliff faces from view, he saw her.

Effie was evidently lying down. Spencer could see her fingers over the edge of the ledge she was looking over. A grin burst over her face. "You found us!"

"Thank God!" Libby clutched Spencer's arm with both hands.

Thunder peeked over the edge. "Yip! Yip!" Backed away.

"I knew you'd find us!"

Spencer wished he'd been as sure. "Are you all right? Have you been hurt?" he called. *Find out about her first, then ask about Evan,* he told himself.

"No, but we can't get down. Evan's over there. He can't get to me, either." She pointed to her left.

Spencer's gaze followed along the narrow ledge that ran in the direction she pointed. *Must be how they got where they are,* he realized. But where was Evan?

"I don't see him." Libby's voice was thick with worry.

He placed a hand over hers, where she still clutched his arm. He moved through the trees in the direction Effie had indicated, trying to watch the cliff as he walked.

He stopped abruptly. Blood drained from his heart.

Instinctively, his arms circled Libby, drawing her against his chest to shield her from the inevitable pain and fright.

Evan stood on the narrow ledge as if his back were glued to the cliff wall. On either side of him, the ledge had slipped away. No more than two feet of ledge was left.

sixteen

"Oh, no!" Libby's horror-filled whisper squeezed Spencer's heart unbearably.

His arms tightened about her. "Evan is safe for now. We'll get him down." *Or I'll die trying,* he promised both of them silently. "No wonder we haven't heard him calling."

"He's probably too frightened to let out a breath."

Evan seemed to be looking in their direction. Spencer wasn't sure whether or not he could see them through the trees. He sensed Libby was about to call to Evan. "We don't want to startle him."

He felt her nod against his shoulder.

He took a deep breath. "Hi, Evan!" he called, trying to keep his voice light and friendly. "Your aunt Libby and I are here. We see you, tadpole! Don't you worry, now. I'm going to get you down. Okay?"

Evan's head barely moved in a nod.

Libby wrapped her hands around one of Spencer's arms again and leaned her head against his shoulder. He felt her shake as she took a breath, and he leaned his cheek briefly against the top of her head, keeping his attention on Evan.

"Give us wisdom, Lord," he heard her whisper, "and keep Evan safe."

Anger surged through him. *I'm the one who has to save Evan, not God!* He tried to push his fury away. Through his years as a steamboat captain, he'd learned that anger had no place in an emergency; it only clouded good judgment.

"Evan," he called, "I'm going down to the rowboat to get a rope. I'll go as fast as I can, I promise. You're doing fine up there. Your aunt Libby's going to stay right here and talk to you until I get back. Okay?"

Again, Evan's head barely moved. "H–hurry!"

Spencer barely caught the word, but his heart constricted at the sound of it. "I'm leaving right now, Evan!" He looked down at Libby. "Talk to him. Talk about anything. Let him keep hearing your voice so he knows he's not alone."

"I will." She released his arm. The terror in her eyes made him want to take her in his arms again and make the fear go away, but the only way he could make it go away was to get those kids down safe.

"You're a strong woman, Libby. You can do it." He turned and started running back the way they'd come, crashing through the trees. *Can Evan hear all the racket I'm making? I hope so. Hope he knows it's the sound of help coming as soon as possible.*

By the time he'd reached the main path, his face and hands were covered with scratches from the branches he'd pushed through. Somewhere he'd lost his hat. He slipped and slid down the path to the river. A couple times he'd thought he'd lose a boot to the mud.

Things weren't any easier at the rowboat. He spent many frustrated minutes trying to undo the knot securing the anchor so he could take the rope back up the hillside. He considered going out to the *Jennie Lee* to try to find a rope, but the rowboat's anchor rope was long and strong, just what he needed.

By the time he got back to Libby, his chest burned and his legs ached from the unusual exertion.

"Captain Matthews is back," Libby called to Evan when Spencer came into her sight.

"Hi, Evan!" Spencer tried to make his voice cheerful. "You're doing fine up there. You've got a better view than any pilot in a pilothouse."

She looked at the rope, then met Spencer's gaze. She looked anxious. "What are you going to do?"

"I don't know yet." Trying to get his panting under control, he stared at the cliff and the trees about them. None of the trees were close enough to Evan or Effie to be of any help. The cliff walls were sheer and treeless. "Don't see how we can get to the kids from here. We'll have to see if we can get to them from up above."

"But how can you do that? The ledge is gone, and it's a straight drop from the top to where the children are."

"I know. We'll have to see what's up there that we can turn to our advantage. How's Evan doing?"

"He's terrified."

"Effie?"

"She's all right. There's a cave behind her, she says, so she isn't in imminent danger like Evan, though she can't climb up or down, either."

"Need to check some things out, Evan," Spencer called. "We won't be talking to you for a couple minutes, but we're still here. We won't leave without you and Effie, I promise."

Spencer headed back toward Effie, trying to study the broken ledge through the trees. If he could somehow reach the cave, maybe he'd be able to find a way to reach Evan from there by an outcropping or by still-intact pieces of ledge.

Nothing looked promising. He tried to ignore the hopelessness that was creeping into his brain and heart, dulling his ability to look for solutions. *Pull yourself together. Giving up won't help.* Maybe he should send Libby back to River's Edge for assistance. It was a long way, but she'd said she'd left the carriage up on the bluff near the road, and—

"That's it!"

"What's it?" Libby held a branch aside as she moved to his side.

"The carriage! I'll tie the rope around myself, tie the other end around the harness shaft. I'll climb down to the kids from the bluff, and the horse will pull us up."

Libby's face went white. "That sounds dangerous."

"Not as dangerous as leaving Evan on that eroding ledge." His steps quickened. "I'll need you to come up top with me to lead the horse."

He stopped again below Effie and called to her that they were going up top. "Be sure to let Evan know, in case he can't hear us."

"Are you leaving?" Effie yelled.

"Not a chance." Spencer could hear the fright in her voice. *More like barely disguised hysteria,* he thought. Not surprising, though he knew there wasn't much that frightened that spunky girl. "I think I'll be able to reach you and Evan better from the top, that's all."

"Why don't you sing some of your favorite songs, Effie?" Libby suggested. "Maybe 'Oh, How I Love Jesus.' "

"Okay."

As he hurried toward the path, Spencer could hear her sweet young voice singing out words that sounded absurd to him under the circumstances: "Oh, how I love Jesus, because He first loved me."

As soon as he came out on top of the bluff, his eyes searched the small clearing. On the far side, the horse, still attached to the carriage, was tied to an oak. "Sweetest sight I've seen in all my years." He glanced at Libby. "Will you get the horse? I'll let the kids know we're here and see if I can find a good place to lower myself over the edge."

She bit her lip, looking worried at his words, but she nodded and started off in a run.

She must be exhausted, he thought, moving along the edge of the bluff, *but she's still running. Must be love for the kids fueling her.*

The horse was young, strong, and best of all, not skittish. "He's from Justin's stables," Libby told him.

He was relieved. He'd expected a horse from a public stable. Usually rather docile animals, but no telling what to expect in strength or willingness to perform some unusual stunt such as he was about to ask.

Quickly, Spencer checked the carriage and its boot.

Libby shifted anxiously. "What are you looking for?"

"Anything that might help us out in the rescue attempt." All he found was a lap robe and a short carriage whip.

Giving up his fruitless search, he started preparations for his climb. He attached one end of the anchor rope to one of the wooden shafts connecting the horse to the carriage and tied the other end around himself, using a strange cradlelike configuration. The rope went around his waist, through his legs, around one thigh, through his belt buckle, back through his legs and around the other thigh. He grinned at Libby. "At least I've learned how to tie a few good knots during my years as a river man."

She almost smiled.

He explained what he wanted her to do, guiding the horse. Fear passed over her already-pale face, followed by determination. She squared her shoulders and looked him right in the eye. "I can do that."

He touched his fingers to her cheek. "I never doubted it. We're going to get those kids up here safe and sound, Libby. We're going to do it together."

She nodded. "Together."

Spencer checked the knots fastening the rope about him one last time. Not that he thought it was necessary, but he didn't think Libby would appreciate it if he was looking her in the face when he asked his next question. "Can I have your petticoat?"

There wasn't an answer. Didn't appear to be any movement, either. At least, the hem of her skirt, easily visible to him, hadn't risen an inch. He glanced up. "Is that a no?"

Her face was no longer pale. "I–I'm not wearing a petticoat." She lifted her skirt about six inches. The bottom of ruffled and bowed pantaloons peeked out cheerfully, though wearing a muddy facial after Libby's trips up and down the bluff path.

He couldn't contain his grin. "Great. Those will do even better. Take them off, will you?" He turned his back.

"Here," she said a minute later. "What. . .what are you going to do with them?"

"Might need something extra to secure Evan to me," he answered, tying them around his waist.

When he was done, he laid his hands on Libby's shoulders. "Ready?"

She bit her lip and nodded. "Be careful."

He fought back the desire to take her in his arms and kiss

her, just in case things didn't work out the way they were supposed to work out, but he didn't want her to sense his fear. He knew that would only make things harder for her.

He settled for giving her a wink.

The thought flashed through his mind that in addition to praying for Evan and Effie, she'd be praying for him while he attempted to rescue the children. It didn't comfort him, but he suddenly understood that her prayers were a way of loving him and the children, a way for her to go beyond her ability to physically help and protect them.

Back at the cliff, he called down over the edge. "I'm coming down, Evan. You don't have to look up. You'll know when I get there."

The thought of stepping back over the edge of the cliff, even with a horse tied to the other end of the rope, was more frightening than Spencer wanted to admit to himself. He hadn't done this in years. Not, in fact, since he'd been a young man and used to slip down over cliffs along this same line of bluffs with his friends—more than thirty-five years ago!

When I came back to River's Edge, I wanted to recapture some of my youth, but this is ridiculous!

"Ready, Libby?"

Standing with her hand on the horse's harness, she nodded.

He took a deep breath, gave Libby a grin, and stepped back into space.

seventeen

Spencer lowered himself down, heart in his throat. He could hear Effie, still singing. A reminder he would be doing this again if. . .no, when, this first mission was accomplished.

He'd told Libby to keep the horse a few feet back from the edge. The horse wasn't lowering Spencer; it would instead be used to pull him and Evan back up. Still, whenever the horse moved, Spencer would drop a couple of feet or be yanked up a couple of feet unexpectedly, sometimes swinging hard against the cliff wall. By the time he was almost to Evan and had called to Libby to stop, his hands were already torn and bruised from the rope and rock.

He saw in a flash it wouldn't be wise to add his weight to Evan's on the remaining piece of ledge. Instead, he walked himself down the wall until he was alongside Evan. "How's the *Jennie Lee*'s future pilot?"

Huge brown eyes beseeched him. "I w–want to g–get down!"

"That's why I'm here. I won't leave without you, I promise." Spencer steeled himself against the boy's terror and the sob-like shaking in his voice. He could see traces of tear trails on Evan's cheeks.

"I'm s–scared!"

"That's all right." Spencer tried to reassure the boy while analyzing the situation. "You've done just what you should. You stayed put, waited for help, didn't move around too much. When a man does what he should do, even when he's scared, he's brave. I'm proud of you, Evan. Now, just let me take a good look at things here, and then we'll get started."

"O–o–kay."

He could feel the boy's eyes watching every move of his eyes. Spencer disciplined his face not to show his emotions.

133

He didn't want the boy to see his fear.

Evan was still pasted to the wall. *Couldn't be closer to it if he'd been sculpted from it,* Spencer thought. Discouragement washed through him. He'd hoped to find a way to secure Evan to himself with Libby's pantaloons, but he could see there wasn't any chance the boy would move his body far enough away from the cliff wall that he could fit the pantaloons around him.

"Here's what we're going to do, Evan. I'm going to step in front of you on that ledge. As soon as I do, I'm going to pick you up. I want you to put your arms around my neck and hold on tight. Then wrap your legs around my waist. Got it?"

Evan nodded.

Spencer knew they'd need to act quickly. He wasn't certain that little piece of rock would hold his weight as well as Evan's, even for a minute. As soon as his boots touched the remaining ledge, he slid both arms to one side of the rope and reached for Evan's waist.

The sound of pebbles bouncing down the cliff below them sent terror spiraling through him.

He yanked Evan up and against his chest. Felt the boy's arms squeeze his neck and the skinny legs wrap around his waist. Evan's chest shook against his own.

Spencer leaned forward until Evan's shoulders were against the wall again. "I'm going to tie you to me before we start up. To do that, I'll have to let go of you for a minute."

"No!" Evan's hold grew impossibly tighter.

"You'll be safer when I'm done. Just hold on tight to me with your arms and legs. Don't let go, no matter what happens."

He felt Evan's nod against his cheek.

Spencer undid the knot at his side. *If that ledge goes before I finish tying him—*

He didn't let himself finish the thought.

Sweat slid down his forehead, stinging his eyes with salt, while he slid a pantaloons leg between Evan's back and the rope. "Hear your sister singing? She has a good voice."

He tried to keep casual talk going to calm Evan somewhat.

"Guess you know how the *Jennie Lee* feels now, stuck on that sandbar unable to go wherever she wants."

The ledge began to shift beneath his feet. His hands stopped. His heart leaped to his throat. He tried to swallow it. Tried again. "How about when we get her off that old sandbar if you and I take her out on the river and I let you take the wheel?"

Voice creaked like an old riverboat in a storm, he thought in disgust, knotting the pantaloons legs to the rope where it was tied about his own waist. With the completion of the knot came a sliver of relief. In case something happened, the pantaloons might give him an extra few seconds to grab the boy and react.

"All done. Ready to go up?"

Evan nodded.

Spencer dropped back his head to call to Libby.

The ground moved beneath his feet.

His stomach turned over.

A moment later, he and Evan dropped through space, coming to a jolting halt six feet below where the ledge had been. Evan's scream rang in Spencer's ear.

Help us, God! I can't save him alone! The words roared in his mind. His arms clenched about the boy. He swung his body to catch the brunt of the blow as they smashed against the cliff. A small shower of dirt and rubble poured over them. He slipped one hand behind Evan's head. "It's all right. I've got you."

A heart was racing faster than floodwaters on the Mississippi. Spencer wasn't sure whether it was his or Evan's. *Both,* he decided.

"Spencer? Evan? Are you all right?"

"We're fine, Libby."

"What happened?"

He ignored her question. "Evan and I are ready to get back up top. Start moving the horse back, slowly."

Even with the horse doing most of the work, it was a long way back up. Spencer kept constant vigil, trying to keep Evan from colliding with the wall.

When they were finally on top, Spencer and Evan collapsed in a pile on the ground. Evan broke into quiet sobs. Libby raced over to them, dropping to her knees, and throwing her arms around them.

A moment later, she was yanking at the knot in the pantaloons that held Evan to Spencer, comforting Evan with soft chatter. Spencer stayed where he was, panting, watching her. Her eyes glittered suspiciously, but she wasn't crying.

His heart swelled with love of her. *You are some woman, Libby.*

He couldn't rest for long. There was still Effie to rescue. After examining the rope to be sure it hadn't been dangerously damaged and checking the knots to ensure they were still secure, he prepared for the next descent.

The ordeal wasn't nearly as trying this time. He and Libby and the horse all knew what they were doing. The ledge in front of the cave where Effie was located appeared strong and secure.

When he landed on it, Effie threw herself against him, wrapping her arms about his waist, almost knocking him off into space. "Captain!"

Steadying himself, he hugged her. "Hi, there, tadpole."

Thunder jumped about, yipping a greeting.

"Ready to go back up top, Effie?"

She let loose her hold and grabbed one of his hands. "First, I want to show you what I found in the cave."

Spencer's laugh boomed out, releasing the tension he hadn't realized had built in his chest muscles. *Trust Effie to be more concerned with adventure than with her own safety! Why, she doesn't appear frightened one whit.*

Effie frowned, touching a row of ruffles on the pantaloons legs tied about his waist. "What's this?"

Briefly, he explained. Then he called up to Libby that Effie was safe and unharmed and that they wouldn't be ready to ascend for a few minutes. He turned to Effie and chuckled. "Did you find the captain's treasure?"

Her brown curls swung as she shook her head. "No."

They didn't have to go far. Just inside the mouth, behind a boulder, she pointed at a jumble of items. "Look!"

Spencer looked. "Picks, chisels, shovels, lanterns, tin buckets, ropes, matches, gunnysacks, even a blanket."

Effie wrinkled her nose. "The blanket's dirty and stinky. I thought I'd bring it out to sit on while I waited for you, but it was too awful."

He peered back into the low-ceilinged cave. Too dark to see anything. He could use the lanterns at his feet to explore further, but he hadn't the desire. Obviously, whoever was responsible for the lights people had been seeing along the bluff cliffs had stored things here. If he weren't exhausted from rescuing Evan and the need to get Effie safely back to the top of the bluff, he might be more inclined to look further into the cave.

He rested a hand on her shoulder. "Quite a find, Effie, but what do you say we get back to the top? Libby and Evan will be worrying about us."

Before heading back out to the ledge, he grabbed the rope from the treasure hunters' pile.

Back outside, Spencer looked out toward the river. He could barely see it through the trees. Treetops would almost completely hide the ledge and cave from view from the river or the opposite bank.

He explained to Effie how he planned to tie her to himself and how the horse would pull them back up. The idea of sliding up a cliff at the end of a rope didn't seem to disturb her a bit.

"Okay." She leaned down and picked up Thunder, who licked her nose. "We're ready."

I hadn't counted on this. "We can't take Thunder, tadpole. It's too dangerous."

She set her mouth in a manner that left no doubt of her intent. "Then I'm not going, either."

Spencer crouched down beside her. "You can't stay here. You know that."

"Neither can Thunder."

She's as stubborn as Libby. "I'll come back for Thunder

after you're safe on top. He'll be safe here until then."

"I want to take him with me."

"I know that, Effie, but what if he slipped?"

"I'll hold him tight."

"Thunder might get scared and wiggle loose from your arms, even though I know you'd do everything you could to hold on to him. You don't want him to fall, do you?"

She didn't answer. Her eyes filled with tears but remained defiant.

"It will be safer for him if I come back for him alone, Effie."

"You won't drop him?"

"I won't drop him."

"Promise?"

"Promise."

Slowly, she knelt down, hugged Thunder tightly, and released him. "Be good, Thunder. Captain Matthews will be back for you in a few minutes." She dropped a kiss on Thunder's forehead, and he rewarded her once again with two quick little licks on the tip of her nose.

Thunder's whine followed them all the way up the cliff.

It wasn't long before Effie was in Libby's arms.

"One more trip," he told Libby.

He could see she didn't like the thought of him going back over the edge for a dog, but after a glance at the children's faces, she didn't argue. When he was back at the cave, he retrieved a gunnysack from the treasure hunters' stash. Thunder objected to being stuffed into it, but Spencer thought he had a better chance of not dropping the dog if he carried him in this manner.

The trip was successful. Effie and Evan, already recovering from his ordeal, fell on the dog as soon as Thunder crawled out of the sack. The little pink tongue worked as fast as the tail in telling the children how glad he was to be with them again.

Joy filled Libby's face as she watched them tumbling about each other.

Just seeing her like this is worth everything it took to save those kids, Spencer thought.

Her shining gaze turned to him and she reached for his hand. "Thank you."

He knew her heart was in those two simple words. He could feel it. She knew he would have rescued those children even if they weren't related to her, even if he didn't even know them. But he understood, too, how important it was to her that they were safe.

He squeezed her hand. "We did it together."

Once the four tired, muddy people and the muddy, still-wiggling dog climbed into the carriage and started toward River's Edge, Spencer asked, "How did you two find that ledge and cave? They're pretty well hidden by the trees."

"Last night we saw lights on the cliffs from the *Jennie Lee,* remember?" Effie asked.

Spencer nodded.

"Well," she continued, "we watched carefully. Then today, we tried to remember where on the cliffs we saw the lights. We tried to find that place. We had to climb around in the trees and rocks a lot, but finally, we found that ledge."

"We knew there were caves in the cliffs," Evan said. "Bandits have hidden things in the caves before."

"Yes," Effie interrupted. "So we just followed the ledge to the cave. Or at least, Thunder and me did. The ledge broke before Evan got to the cave." She gasped and turned quickly in her seat. "Evan, I almost forgot to tell you what I found in the cave!"

It took several minutes for Effie to tell Libby and Evan what she found, as she embellished the telling in her usual dramatic storytelling manner.

"Of course," she concluded, "it would have been better if we'd found the treasure or the treasure hunters."

Libby gasped.

Spencer reached for her hand. He knew what she was thinking; that if the treasure hunters had been there, they might have endangered the children further. "They weren't there," he reminded her in a low voice, not meant to carry to the children in the backseat.

"What?"

"Nothing, Effie."

Effie hung over the front of the seat between Spencer and Libby. "At least we proved one thing."

"What's that?" Libby asked.

"It's not a ghost carrying those old lanterns around. A ghost wouldn't need real lanterns, would he?"

"No, he wouldn't," Libby agreed. "Constance and Justin will be glad to know you found out it's people and not ghosts."

The children were quiet for a couple minutes. Finally, Effie spoke up in the most insecure tone Spencer had heard from her yet. "Do you think we need to tell Aunt Constance and Uncle Justin what happened?"

Spencer looked down at his chest and lap. The color of his clothes was barely discernable through the mud. He saw Libby's gaze following the same path, her eyes twinkling.

"Oh, yes, Effie." Libby smiled. "I don't think you can hide this one."

☙

A couple hours later, after delivering the children home and explaining the situation to Justin and Constance, Spencer and Libby left the reunited family. Justin had kindly allowed them the use of his carriage for Spencer to take Libby home. Even in its confines, Libby was self-conscious about her mud-splattered appearance as they drove through town.

Don't be silly, she scolded herself. *The children are safe. What does it matter what people think of the way I look?*

She glanced at Spencer out of the corner of her eye. She'd been terrified she'd lose the children and Spencer, too, out on those cliffs. *Thank You, Lord, for saving them.*

Her glance dropped to his hands, which held the reins lightly. His hands were torn and bruised, dried blood mixed with mud covered them. Her heart contracted. All that painful damage caused by saving her niece and nephew.

She reached out and grasped the reins. "I'll drive."

He gave her a curious look. "I can drive."

"I know, but you needn't. I shouldn't have let you drive all this way with your hands as they are. They must hurt awfully."

He let her take the reins but didn't reply immediately. Finally he said, "They're beginning to throb. I didn't notice too much at first."

"When we get to my place, we'll wash and bandage them."

The sound of the carriage wheels and the horse's hooves and the noise of children playing in the early evening filled the silence between them for a few minutes.

They were only a couple blocks from her home when he cleared his throat. "I prayed up there, Libby, trying to save Evan. For the first time in thirty-five years, I prayed."

Joy and hope flooded her. The energy the day's events had sapped came roaring back. She turned to meet his gaze. "You did?"

"I did. But you know something? You and I were the only ones helping that boy. I didn't see God reaching down to help out."

Pain replaced the joy that had filled her moments earlier. What could she say to him? He'd cried out to God on that cliffside. Even so, he wouldn't admit to himself that God had given him the wisdom and strength to save Evan, that God had left that little bit of path for Evan when the rest of the path slid down the bluff.

But he'd prayed. The words whispered through her mind. *Somewhere, deep inside, beyond his logical mind perhaps, he'd realized he needed God's help.*

She pulled the carriage alongside the carriage stoop in front of her cottage, driving carefully. She didn't drive often; she walked most places.

"I see Daniel's here again."

At Spencer's comment, Libby looked past him to the house. Ida and Pastor Green sat on the front porch. Libby lifted the watch set in a sterling silver heart pinned on her bodice and groaned. "I invited him to dinner tonight. I'd forgotten all about it."

"There was a time I would have found that encouraging. You're late for another evening with Daniel, and I'm escorting you while he waits."

She darted Spencer a dirty look. Her gaze and her attitude were stopped abruptly by the sad look in his eyes and his equally sad, small smile.

"Daniel is a good man, Libby. I don't see how you could do better. You should start treating him with more respect."

Without waiting for an answer, he climbed down from the carriage, then turned to help her down.

Libby felt as though burning coals filled her stomach. Her emotions were in a jumble. She was in no mood to answer all the questions she knew Ida and Pastor Green would pose when they saw the state of her and Spencer's clothing. All she wanted was to finish this discussion with Spencer.

What did he mean, saying those things about Daniel, Lord? She was terribly afraid he had meant he was giving up on her, giving up on the dream of them. Of course, she couldn't marry him, anyway, if he didn't love God, but. . .if he was giving up on them, was he closing the door forever on God, too? *I don't want him to close the door on either of us!*

eighteen

A couple days later, Spencer stopped into the *Jennie Lee*'s dining hall to check on his hired help. Adams's lean body moved rhythmically while he scrubbed the salon walls with a brush and hot, soapy water.

"You're doing good work, Adams."

Adams stopped his rhythm to grin at him. "Glad to do it. Not exactly the kind of work I'm accustomed to, but I kinda like helpin' ta bring this lady back ta her old good looks."

Spencer smiled. "Me, too." *Men who love boats and the river are always alike beneath the skin,* he thought.

He wandered out onto the deck, noticing along the way the myriad of things that needed shining or cleaning or repairing or painting. Good thing he'd hired Adams. Sometimes he regretted having someone else on board. Never knew when the man would walk in on him. Still, he couldn't get any work done by himself right now.

He lifted his bandaged hands, rested the backs of them against the railing, and looked out over the river. Rope burns, blisters, and cuts and scrapes from the cliff rocks had turned his hands into swollen, useless appendages. It would be a week or so, the doctor said, until they lost their tenderness to the point he could get along without the bandages.

He was stiff all over, too. "Move like an old man," he complained.

Leaning against the railing, he sighed deeply. The familiar refrain of the river running past the *Jennie Lee* accompanied his memories of that day on the cliff. He'd relived that day more often than he'd like to admit, both waking and sleeping.

The story of the day's events had spread through River's Edge faster than water flows over a dam. He was considered the town's local hero. He snorted. A hero wasn't anyone but someone who did what needed to be done. What alternatives did a person have? It was almost humiliating, being treated as if he'd done something special. Did people think he and Libby could have left those children to try to save themselves?

He'd been deeply shaken by the events of that day. *Even fighting wild river currents and storms, I've never felt so helpless as when I saw Evan on the side of that bluff.*

Something different shook him now that Evan and Effie were safe. As a riverboat captain, he'd relied on his own knowledge and logic to save himself and his boats and passengers through the years. *This time, I know You intervened, God.*

He wasn't ready to admit it to anyone else, *especially* to Libby. He could barely admit it to himself and God yet.

"So, where do we go from here, God?"

Later that day, he dug out the Bible he'd seen before in the captain's quarters. He couldn't remember the last time he'd opened a Bible. Probably back before he married.

"Humph! Was nothing more than a fool kid. Now that I've a few years on me, I've learned how little I knew about just about everything back then. Why should I have thought my beliefs about God were any more accurate than anything else I believed then?"

When he finally located the book, he took it outside, settled himself in a wooden deck chair in the sunshine, and opened it up. He'd been in church enough times throughout his life that he wasn't completely ignorant of the book. "Maybe I'll start with John. That's where that verse pastors are always quoting, John 3:16, is from: 'For God so loved the world, that he gave his only begotten Son, that whosoever believeth in him should not perish, but have everlasting life.' " He was a little surprised at the ease with which the verse he'd memorized as a boy came back to him.

He started at the beginning of John. He was still reading when Adams came up two hours later.

"How about if I catch some fish and prepare some lunch for us, Captain?"

"Thanks. I have some bread in my cabin we can have with the fish."

Loaves and fishes, he thought, amused, as he watched Adams leave. Then he turned back to the book. "Don't remember the Bible being this interesting when I was a youngster," he murmured.

He couldn't get enough of it. For the next few days, he was reading it every spare moment—and he had a lot of spare moments.

Adams was helping all over the boat now. On Friday, Spencer looked over some of the work he'd done and was pleased with it. "This isn't one of the most elegant paddle wheelers," he told Adams, "but it must have been a beauty when it was new."

"They always are, aren't they?" Adams agreed. "How about if I wash and wax the floor in your quarters? It was lookin' pretty bad last time I was up there."

"That's a good idea. By the way, I heard the *Spartan* has headed north. Should reach here in a few days."

"That's good news."

"I'm sure you'll be glad to get back to your old boat, but I'm going to miss your help around here."

Adams grinned his lazy grin. "Thanks. Water's risin' every day. Expect it'll be high enough soon to let the *Jennie Lee* float free. Found another place to beach her?"

"I'm going to try to rent a place at the landing in River's Edge."

Adams nodded. "Well, I'd best get started on that floor." He headed off.

Spencer walked about the boat, pleased with all that had been started on his restoration project.

"Must be how You feel about us, God." He'd fallen into the practice of talking to God often now, both out loud and silently. "I used to think religion was nothing but a theory and acts and rules, but it's not. You reach out to us and offer to repair the battered places in our souls, like I'm trying to repair this boat." He looked around and took a deep breath. "Well, God, I believe in Your Son, now, like John 3:16 says we must. I'd like You to come into my life and fix *my* battered places."

࿇

Libby wasn't surprised to see Spencer at church Sunday. He'd been there every Sunday since he arrived in River's Edge. But she hadn't forgotten his words about God not helping to save the children. A wave of hopelessness washed over her when she saw him sit down at the end of the pew beside Evan. *Please, Lord, don't give up on him,* she prayed again.

Effie stood up and moved from between Evan and Libby to the other side of Spencer. Libby and Constance shared a smile at the girl's actions. The children had taken to Spencer from the start. The events of the day on the cliff had given him a permanent place in their hearts.

Though the service was starting, the children were whispering eagerly to him. Libby could guess what they were saying. They wanted to spend the afternoon at the steamboat.

The introductory music stopped, and Libby could hear Effie's plea.

"We'll bring the lunch to thank you for saving us," Effie told him. "It's all ready. We brought the picnic basket. It's in the carriage. All you have to do is say yes."

Spencer's eyes twinkled. "Yes." Then he pointed to the front, where Pastor Green was speaking, indicating the children should stop talking.

Evan and Effie grinned at each other over Spencer's lap. Then Effie looked at Libby and formed her fingers into an "O," signifying everything was okay for the picnic.

After the service, the children hurried to Libby's side. "Captain Matthews said we can go to the *Jennie Lee* for a picnic. Let's hurry."

"Am I invited, too?"

"Of course!" Effie assured her. "It's a thank-you picnic for saving us, and you helped."

"She sure did," Spencer agreed.

Libby returned his smile. "The bandages are off your hands."

"Yes. They're still sore, but I can do most everyday things now if I'm careful. I can't row, though. That's too demanding."

"How will we get to the boat if you can't row?" Evan's voice was thick with disappointment.

"Adams, the man who is living on my boat and helping me out, rowed me into town for church. I'm sure he won't mind rowing us back out."

It was a pleasant trip out to the boat. She hadn't felt so relaxed around Spencer since he arrived in River's Edge. Something had changed. He seemed more peaceful, more settled, not as determined to push his way onto her. *Is it because he's given up on us, Lord? Please, don't let it be that!*

Once they'd boarded, the children's attention turned to the subject that had interested them for weeks.

"Have you seen any lights on the bluffs, Captain?" Evan asked.

"Not since you two found the cave. Expect the treasure hunters haven't been able to get to their lanterns since the ledge is broken."

The children, restless as ever, wanted to move around a bit before they ate. "Can we go to the pilothouse?" Evan begged. Spencer gave permission, and the twins headed for the pilothouse. Libby and Spencer watched them run down the deck, laughing.

"You look especially nice today, Libby. I like that hat."

"Thank you." It was a new little number that she especially liked. A feminine, low-crowned derby style with a wide green ribbon that matched her outfit around the crown and tied in a large bow at one side. Two pheasant feathers stuck perkily out of the bow.

"Would you like to see how much work has been done on the place since you were here last?" Spencer asked.

Libby nodded. "Very much."

The dining hall looked worse than before, with the drapes down. The brass, however, shone. "I need to paper this room," he told her. "Haven't chosen any yet. I'm not very good at things like that."

"I'd be glad to help you select some, if you'd trust my judgment."

"Of course, I trust your judgment." Hands in his trouser pockets, he surveyed the long room. "A lot of decorating to be done. We'll need new draperies, upholstery, rugs, and likely things I'm not remembering. It will mean not only deciding on fabric, but hiring someone to make the items." He turned to her. "Would you help with those, too?"

She hesitated. She'd never decorated anything but her small home and her millinery shop. To decorate the hall sounded like such fun, but it also seemed an intimate thing to do for him and would require them spending a lot of time together. She loved spending time with him all together too much. It was time she put a halt to it.

"I'm sorry, Libby. I forgot for a moment that you have the shop to run. You don't have time to take on my projects."

Perhaps it was safer to allow him to believe his interpretation of her hesitation was correct than to destroy his friendliness this afternoon with the truth. The end result would be the same. "I will help with the wallpaper if you still wish it. Also, I can suggest someone to help with the rest."

They talked for a few minutes about colors and styles that he liked.

"What are you going to do with the *Jennie Lee* when you're finished restoring her?" Libby asked. "Surely you aren't going to live on her the rest of your life. It's a rather large home for one person."

Immediately she wished she could bite back her words. It sounded as though she were suggesting he ask her to marry him again!

If he thought so, he pretended not to notice. "I wasn't sure what I'd do with her when I started. Guess I thought my company—my sons' company now—could use another boat, though with the growth of railroads, steamboat travel is down to a trickle. Nothing to be done to turn the tide of progress back. Travel by rail is faster and, of course, tracks can be laid where rivers don't run."

"The change to railroads is too bad, I think, at least for passengers." Libby ran a fingertip along a brass bar that added a decorative point to the wall. "Steamboat travel is so much more luxurious and relaxing."

"I think so, too."

His voice had that gentle quality to it that it so often had when something they shared was discussed. Libby liked the way shared beliefs about even something this simple made her feel a warm connection with him. *I can only imagine how close we'd feel if we shared a faith in Christ.*

"The last few days," Spencer was continuing, "I've been thinking about the decline in steamboat travel. I'd like to put the *Jennie Lee* back in service, catering to people who want to enjoy the more leisurely form of travel for relatively short distances on the river; maybe from Prairie du Chien to St. Paul, for instance. It's a small boat, as paddle wheelers go. It would be a good size for that kind of service. What do you think?"

"It sounds like a lovely idea."

"Or maybe I'll move back to St. Louis and run the boat from there. The running season is pretty well year around below St. Louis."

Libby's blood seemed to freeze at his words. *Leave? I might never see him again!* Frustration at her ambivalence made her impatient with herself. Hadn't she just told herself she should stop spending time with him? *But to never see him again! Lord, I'm not ready for that.* Would she ever be?

"Be near the boys and their families in St. Louis, too," Spencer said.

"Yes. It's good to be near family. I wouldn't want to be away from Constance and the children." Her lips felt numb. All of her felt numb.

"I've discovered I'm not very good at this retirement business. Guess that's why I took on this project with the *Jennie Lee.* I could keep my hand in with the packet company I started if I chose, but I believe it's important for my boys to learn to run the business themselves. They're going to have some rough years ahead with changes in travel, but learning to make it through rough times is what makes a man."

What rough times is he thinking of from his own life? Libby wondered. *Those of his personal life or those from his business life that I don't know about?*

He took her elbow. "There are some changes I'd like to make in the captain's quarters, too. Would you mind looking at it with me and seeing what you think of my ideas?"

She nodded, still numb from his news, and allowed him to escort her out of the dining hall and toward the cabin.

The captain's quarters were quietly elegant. The rich paneling and walnut furnishings made it a beautiful room, in a manly sense. To Libby, it seemed a room in which Spencer would feel completely comfortable.

Although she'd seen the room before when Spencer had given her and the children a tour of the boat, she was looking at it with different eyes now that Spencer wanted her advice on making changes.

She stopped before the huge walnut desk and leather chair. On the desk lay an open Bible.

Spencer was talking, spelling out his dissatisfactions with the room and his ideas for changes. The words didn't register to Libby. The Bible had all her attention.

Has he been reading it? After all the times he's railed against God and my faith in Him, why is he reading it? She couldn't reconcile the act with the man she knew. A tiny flame of hope flickered in her chest. *You haven't given up on him, have You, Lord? Thank You!*

Would Spencer be upset if she asked him about the open Bible? She couldn't remember a time they'd discussed faith when he hadn't become irate. She didn't want to ruin their camaraderie this afternoon, but she could barely stand her curiosity. She screwed up her courage.

"Spencer," she said, interrupting his comments on window coverings, "have you been reading the Bible?" She rested her fingertips on the open pages.

He hesitated. "Yes."

Her heart hammered fiercely. "Why?"

Spencer jammed his fists into his jacket pockets. "Remember that I told you I prayed up there on the cliffs when I was rescuing Evan?"

"Yes." She remembered, too, that he'd been adamant that only the two of them, and not God, had helped the children.

"I guess that was the start of realizing I need Him."

Her heart leaped.

He went on, explaining that he'd been reading the Bible all week and that he'd asked God to take over his life. "Reading the Bible, I discovered I'm not the white knight I've always thought. It's true enough that I don't swear or womanize or steal or kill or even drink since my marriage. I always thought that meant I was a good man. But since asking God to restore me to wholeness, I've begun to realize there are many rotten parts of my nature, just as there are often rotten boards in less obvious places on a boat that need replacing. One of the most rotten boards in my own constitution is my pride, my belief in my self-sufficiency."

Libby's heart sang with thankfulness and joy. Her prayer of thirty-five years had been answered!

Spencer moved closer to her. He leaned one hip against the desk. His fingers played with the pages of the Bible, and his gaze watched them.

"You look troubled, Spencer. I would have thought accepting the Lord into your life would give you peace." *Didn't he accept You after all, Lord?*

"When I returned to River's Edge, Libby, and you told me you still wouldn't marry me if I didn't share your faith, I decided to pretend I shared it. My plan was to join the church, become involved in it, and eventually let you think that through the church, I'd become a Christian. But it didn't work that way."

"What do you mean?" She wasn't sure she wanted to know, but she couldn't bear not to.

"In the end, I didn't seek God because of my love for you after all. I sought Him because I recognized I need Him."

Relief dissolved the niggling doubts. She laid a hand over his fingers, where they rested on the Bible's pages. "That's the way it should be, Spencer. It's the only way it can be."

He lifted his gaze to meet hers, and she gave him her biggest smile. "I'm so glad for you, Spencer."

He seemed at a loss for words.

"Oh, I almost forgot!" Libby dug into her drawstring handbag. "I meant to give it to you after church, but when the children invited us to picnic with them, I forgot." She pulled the item out, its weight and smoothness familiar to her hand. "This is something *you* forgot, years ago." *Will he recognize it?* she wondered, laying a small wooden goose in his hand.

He did recognize it. She could tell by the emotions that were working across his weathered face. "The goose. You kept it all these years."

"I kept both of them. The other's still at home on my bureau."

"They're a pair." His voice was low and quiet. "They're meant to be together."

"Do. . .do you want the other one, too?" She hoped not. She had always treasured that special gift.

"No. No, Libby. You keep it." He set the goose on his desk. "Thank you for bringing this one back to me."

The cabin door banged open.

Libby jumped at the sound. She relaxed instantly when Effie and Evan rushed inside.

Evan collapsed into the desk chair. "We're hungry. Can we eat now?"

"What's for lunch?" Spencer asked with a grin.

Effie ticked the items off on her fingers. "Fried chicken, biscuits, strawberry jam, and chocolate cake. We don't need a fire to cook anything, so can we eat on the boat?"

They ate in wooden deck chairs. The children thought it great fun.

"Tell us more stories about lost treasure," Evan begged.

Libby met Spencer's laughing eyes and knew they were thinking the same thing. "I should think you and Effie would have had your fill of treasure stories after your adventure."

"We didn't find any treasure," Effie reminded them, "only tools and stuff."

"Yes," Evan agreed. "Please tell us more stories."

"All right." Spencer swung his feet over the side of his deck chair. He rested his elbows on his knees and leaned forward. "There's a story old river men tell about a race between two paddle wheelers back in '37." He grinned. "That's even before I was born. Below St. Louis, the *Ben Sharrod* overtook *The Prairie*. Well, *The Prairie* didn't want to be passed, so they stoked their boilers and the race was on."

The children forgot their food and listened to his tale, wide-eyed.

He's as much a storyteller as Effie, Libby thought in amusement. But she wasn't interested in lost treasure. With the children involved in Spencer's story, she allowed her mind to explore the issue that had been nagging at her since Spencer shared his new faith with her.

Why had he waited to tell her about his faith until she asked about the open Bible? Why hadn't he told her at the first opportunity? He knew the only reason she had ever given for not marrying him was that he didn't love God.

Has he decided he doesn't love me after all, Lord? she asked silently, not sure she wanted to know the truth. It had been difficult enough to face the prospect of life without Spencer even when she knew he didn't share her faith and she was sure they would never marry. She was glad for his faith, but her heart sank at the thought that he might not love her. Somehow, it seemed more difficult to accept knowing he had turned to God, that now they could share the most important part of their lives together.

But he hadn't brought up the subject of marriage today. Even when she had given him the goose, he had said the two geese were meant to be together, but he didn't say, as he had when he showed her the geese the first time thirty-five years ago, that Spencer and she were meant to be together, too.

Why, he even spoke of possibly moving back to St. Louis! Leaving River's Edge. Leaving me! The thoughts brought tears to her eyes. She tried to blink them back. It wouldn't do to cry in front of the children. She couldn't stop the burning lump that filled her throat.

She watched him now, his face animated in telling his story. The children hung on his every word.

He was part of all of their worlds now.

"One of the survivors of the explosion of the *Sharrod* was found fifteen miles downriver."

"Fifteen miles?" Evan's eyebrows raised.

"Fifteen miles," Spencer assured him. "He was traveling from Louisiana upriver to open a bank. He'd had with him one hundred thousand dollars in gold in two strong boxes."

Evan gasped.

"What happened to it?" Effie asked.

Spencer shrugged, lifted his hands, palms up, and leaned back in his deck chair. "It's at the bottom of the Mississippi. It was never found."

"Wow!" Evan's eyes were still huge.

"Wow," said a voice behind Libby's chair.

She jerked upright and turned to see who it was. "Oh, hello, Mr. Adams." Libby wondered who the burly, redheaded man with him was. The plaid flannel shirts and heavy denim trousers the men wore were in sharp contrast to the Sunday outfits Libby, Spencer, and the children were wearing.

"Something you and your friend wanted, Adams?" Spencer asked pleasantly.

Adams grinned his easygoing grin. He moved casually to stand behind Effie's chair. His hands gripped the back of it behind Effie's head. "Matter of fact, there is, Captain. Too bad about that gold at the bottom of the Mississippi you were talkin' 'bout. But my friend here and me, we're more interested in the treasure the *Jennie Lee*'s captain left behind. We were hopin' you could lead us to it."

"Me? I don't know anything about that treasure."

Adams nodded, still smiling. "Figured you'd say that. Problem is, I don't believe you. Maybe you want ta think 'bout that answer." As calmly as though he were reaching for his handkerchief, he pulled a pistol from behind his waist and pointed it at the back of Effie's head.

Libby went cold all the way to her bones.

nineteen

Fear flooded Spencer. He clenched the arms of the deck chair. His mind felt like a cotton ball. *God, help us!* he cried silently.

The burly man behind Libby pushed back his jacket and pulled out another gun. He said nothing, only pointed the pistol at Libby.

Spencer could only stare in horror. *This can't be happening!*

Even Effie seemed frozen to her chair, her gaze glued to Adams's gun. *Thank You, God! This is no time for her usual daredevil manner.*

Evan's eyes were as large as the paddle wheel. His face was pale as a winter moon.

Adams leaned his forearms on the back of Effie's chair, the end of his pistol dangling perilously close to her head. "Now, what were you sayin', Captain?"

Adams frightened him more than the man beside him. Adams still wore that friendly, good-old-boy smile. His friend had the cold, hard eyes one would expect from a person in this situation.

Spencer forced words past his tongue, which seemed to have swollen in his fear. "What makes you think I know anything about the former captain's treasure?"

Adams shook his head slowly. "Captain, you disappoint me, thinkin' I'm so lackin' in brains. Who'd be stupid enough to fix up this old boat without an ulterior motive? Got to thinkin' 'bout all the time you were spendin' out here. Figured you were lookin' for that dead captain's gold. Now, see, I signed on here to help you so I could get a better look-see on board. Figured Jake here and me could find the treasure ourselves. We didn't want ta resort ta the guns unless it was necessary."

Adams went on to tell all the places he'd searched on the boat while working for Spencer. Spencer paid scant attention to his words. His mind was racing.

He'd wasted his life living for himself instead of the Lord. Now that he'd asked the Lord into his life, would everything end here, for himself and Libby and Effie and Evan? It mustn't!

Show me what to do, God! He sent the plea heavenward.

When there was a break in Adams's story, Spencer spoke up. "If you thought the treasure was on board, why have you and Jake been searching the cliffs at night?"

As usual, Adams was the one who answered. Jake still hadn't opened his mouth. "Well, truth be told, Jake and me didn't think 'bout the possibility it might be on this old boat at first. Took you movin' out here to make us see that. Just in case we were wrong, we kept searchin' the bluffs, too." He waved his pistol back and forth between Effie and Evan in a manner that sent blood pounding through Spencer's veins. "That is, till these two wrecked the path to the cave."

"The rain wrecked it, not us."

Effie's indignant protest made Spencer's hair stand on end in fear for her. "Quiet, Effie!"

His sharp reproval brought a darting glance from her. She shifted slightly but said nothing.

"I always figured the late captain's treasure was nothing more than a rumor." Spencer tried to stall for time. How could he make a treasure materialize when he had no idea if it even existed? How could he fight off these men without a weapon. "There's certainly stories in abundance of treasure lost and hidden along this river, from the beginning of it to the end of it."

Adams cocked back his pistol hammer. He kept the gun aimed on Effie. "You were sayin'?"

Libby gasped.

Don't get hysterical on me, Libby! The memory of her steel nerves during the rescue of the children gave him a sliver of comfort. If a woman had to be in this situation with him, he was glad it was Libby. *Steady, Libby. Keep your wits about you.*

Adams straightened his arm until the pistol's nozzle was less than an inch from Effie's forehead. He didn't say a word—

only kept smiling at Spencer and then raised his eyebrows.

Blood pounded in Spencer's ears. "All right, I'll tell you!"

The words were out before he even thought.

Adams moved the pistol back but kept it aimed at Effie. "Thought you might."

Now what? Spencer cast about for an inkling of an idea to get them out of this nightmare.

"Well?" Adams encouraged.

"He ain't goin' to tell us." Jake's voice was almost a growl. "Mebbe we should show him we mean business."

Spencer flung out an arm. "It's in the captain's quarters!"

Jake finally smiled. "Now that's more like it."

Adams shook his head. "I searched the captain's quarters. Didn't see nothin' that looked like treasure."

Spencer felt like his mind was throwing out fishing lines in every direction, looking for an answer to convince Adams he was telling the truth. "The treasure's not there. It's a map."

"Didn't see no maps, neither."

"It was in with some river charts," Spencer assured him quickly.

Jake and Adams exchanged grins.

"Let's go see it." Adams made a motion with his pistol. "All of you get up, slowlike. Don't try anything brave."

They stood up. Libby started to slip an arm around Effie's shoulders.

"Now, don't be doin' that, ma'am," Adams warned. "You and the captain lead the way. The two younguns will bring up the rear with Jake and me."

Libby's gaze searched out Spencer's. The fear in her eyes almost made him wild. *Remember our God,* he encouraged her silently.

Evan's legs were shaking so badly that Spencer wasn't sure the boy would be able to walk.

Spencer forced his voice to be calm. "Don't worry, tadpoles. Just do as the men tell you."

He found his own legs weren't working too well as he moved toward Libby. His knees had no more thickening than the strawberry jam they'd had with their biscuits for lunch. He had no idea what he was going to do once he got to the cabin. His only hope was that he would spot something there or along the way that he could use for a weapon.

"Hold it!"

At Jake's bark, Spencer and Libby stopped. *What now?* Spencer thought in despair.

Jake undid his belt and yanked it off. He handed his pistol to Adams, then approached Spencer. "Put your hands behind your back."

Spencer followed orders, and Jake used his belt to fasten Spencer's hands together. Spencer's heart dropped to his boots. Now what chance did he have of saving them?

Next the men began belting Libby's hands in front of her. The flame of Spencer's hope died back even more.

Libby winced as Jake pulled the belt tight.

Effie stamped her foot. Her hands were balled into fists at her side. "Don't hurt my aunt Libby, you old mean man, you!"

The men only laughed at her.

"It's all right, dear," Libby assured her. "They didn't hurt me."

That's my girl! Spencer thought. His hope began to lift again. With Libby and Effie's courage to inspire him, he couldn't give up yet.

They passed along the deck and up the steps to the texas.

Maybe it wasn't so smart after all, heading for the cabin, Spencer thought desperately. *If we'd stayed on deck, there'd at least have been a chance a passerby would spot us. There are always a lot of people out fishing and pleasure-boating on a nice Sunday afternoon.*

Too late to change his mind now.

Inside the cabin, Spencer cast about for something, anything, to help them.

"Well, where's this map?" For the first time, he heard impatience in Adams's voice.

Nothing to do but stall for more time. "There's a hidden panel in the wall above the desk, beside that picture of a ship in a storm."

Jake stuck his gun in the waist of his trousers and examined the panel. Nothing happened. He grunted. "This a trick?"

Spencer explained how to open it. While Jake worked at it, Spencer cast about for something, anything, to help them. When the panel was open, and Adams and Jake discovered there was no map, it might all be up for them. If the thieves shot them and left them in the cabin, it might be weeks before their bodies were found.

Nothing looked helpful. His heart sank like an anchor.

Don't give up yet! As long as you're alive, there's a chance. You have to save the twins! His glance slid to them.

He'd expected to see the fear that had been on their faces while on the deck. Instead, they were exchanging conspiratorial grins. He swallowed a groan. *What now?* He wanted to warn them not to do anything foolish, but he didn't want to draw the men's attention to them.

"Eureka!" Jake hollered as the panel slid open. He began pulling out the contents and piling them on the desk, right on top of the open Bible. Spencer knew the papers were mostly old river charts and journals.

Adams stepped behind the desk, keeping the pistol trained on the group, trying to glance at the papers. Jake began going through them. Adams couldn't resist giving a little more of his attention to the pile, too.

Effie dashed toward the open cabin door. She almost lost her balance the last couple feet, sliding on the floor Adams had waxed earlier in the week, her arms flailing.

Evan was right behind her. He almost ran into her. His hands on her back steadied her.

Spencer almost yelled at them to stop. Caught the yell back just in time. Glanced at the desk. All the men's attention was on the pile of papers. *Please, God!* It was all the prayer his mind could form in his fear for what would happen to the children if the men saw them.

Effie had her balance back. She and Evan started again.

"Hey!" Jake let out a bellow. "Stop those kids!"

twenty

Swearing, Adams started after them.

Spencer watched with his heart in his throat. Adams's gun pointed wildly in one direction and then another as he raced across the room.

"Run, Effie! Run, Evan!" Libby screamed.

Effie was through the door. Spencer saw the hem of her dress disappear as she took off down the deck.

"Help! Help!"

She's yelling at the top of her lungs, bless her!

Adams was almost on top of Evan. Spencer held his breath, silently urging Evan to hurry. Adams lost his footing on the slippery floor and landed on his bottom. He reached and caught Evan's jacket just as Evan reached the threshold. They fell in a heap on the floor.

Jake let out a stream of oaths and pushed aside the desk chair, leaving his search to help Adams.

Libby swung her belted hands and shoved the pile of papers onto the floor in front of him.

Jake slipped. Only by grabbing the desk did he manage not to wind up on the floor like his partner.

"Let me go!" Evan was struggling to get away from Adams. His feet and hands were pounding the outlaw with a vengeance. "Let me go!"

"Stupid kid!" Adams tried to subdue Evan while dodging the blows and hanging on to the gun.

Spencer threw himself on top of Adams. He landed with a thud that knocked his breath away. Adams tried unsuccessfully to heave him off and still hold on to the boy and the gun.

Adams's gun arm was behind Spencer. Spencer strained his neck to look over his shoulder. "Oof!" He reached for the gun. Too far away. He grabbed Adams's arm and hung on until Adams yanked so hard Spencer thought his shoulders would come right out of their joints.

He let go and rolled backward over Adams's gun arm. *If I can't get the gun, at least I can keep him from using it.* He was face-to-face with Adams now, and Adams wasn't smiling any longer.

"Stop!" Jake's voice roared through the room.

Spencer glanced up. Jake was standing only a couple feet away, his pistol pointed at Spencer. The sense of failure washed through Spencer.

"Get up."

With an effort, Spencer started to roll off Adams's arm.

"Yipes!"

Jake's gun dropped to the floor.

Libby bent and grabbed it. Trained it on Jake.

Jake, holding his gun hand with his other hand, took a step toward her.

"Stop." Libby took a step back, cocking the pistol's hammer.

Jake looked at her uncertainly.

"Think I won't shoot?" Libby's gaze was steady and so were her still-belted hands. "When you and Adams have been threatening Effie and Evan?"

Jake's shoulders sagged in defeat.

Still on Adams's arm, Spencer grinned. *I'd stop, too, if she used that tone, even without a gun pointed at me.*

"Let go of Evan," she commanded Adams.

Adams released the boy.

"And the gun," she added.

Adams let go of the gun. Spencer could feel Adams give up, as the thief's muscles lost their tension.

"What did you do to Jake?" Spencer asked Libby.

"Stuck my hat pin in his gun hand."

Spencer chuckled. "Evan, pick up Adams's gun." He didn't want to chance the outlaws getting the drop on them again. "But be very, very careful. Don't touch it near the trigger. Hold it in both hands."

When Evan had done as he was told, Spencer explained to

him how to lower the hammer. "Now, take it out on deck and lay it down."

Evan stepped through the door onto the texas deck. "Hey, there's people coming on board from a rowboat!"

"Effie's calls for help must have been answered," Libby said.

Spencer smiled at her across the room, across the two men who had held their lives and the children's in their hands, and thought, *My cries for help were answered, too. How did I ever think I was self-sufficient for all those years?*

Spencer rolled off Adams's arm and struggled to his feet. Evan began undoing the belt that tied his hands together.

They could hear people outside, hear their footsteps running up the steps.

Adams dragged himself to a sitting position. "Could we just see the map? Would you show it to me? We deserve that much after all the trouble we've been through to get it, don't you think?"

Spencer grinned. "There is no map. Far as I know, there never was. I was just stalling for time."

Adams groaned and dropped his head into his hands.

The fishermen Effie had haled helped Spencer tie up Adams and Jake. Then one of the fishermen went into town for the sheriff. When the sheriff had left with Adams and Jake, the fishermen rowed Spencer, Libby, and the twins back to town, where Spencer and Libby brought the children home.

Effie and Evan could barely hold themselves to Spencer and Libby's slower pace. When they reached the block on which they lived, they raced ahead, eager to tell Justin and Constance how they'd help capture the treasure hunters.

There was nothing for it but that Spencer and Libby stay for coffee and straighten out the children's embellished story. Before Spencer left to walk Libby home, Constance invited him to stay with them overnight if he couldn't find someone to take him back to the *Jennie Lee.*

Blossoming spring trees and flowers filled the air with fragrance as Spencer and Libby walked to her home in the twilight.

"You're rather quiet this evening, Libby."

"It's been quite a day."

"That it has. You were incredible."

"Me?"

He laughed. "Yes, you. If you hadn't stuck Jake with that hat pin, no telling what might have happened."

His praise warmed her heart. "This is the third time you've rescued my great-niece and nephew. You are the one who is incredible." She shook her head, unable to find the words she wanted. "I don't know how to thank you."

"There's nothing for which to thank me."

"But that's what is so. . .overwhelming. That it is so much a part of you to be that kind of man."

Spencer chuckled. "Justin and Constance probably don't see me through your eyes. I expect whenever they see me coming up the walk, they tremble with dread, knowing their children have been up to something life-threatening again."

"It does seem their lives go from one traumatic event to the next with surprising speed, doesn't it?"

"If my two boys had sought out trouble the way Effie and Evan do, I'd have been an old man by the time I was thirty."

"You will never seem old to me." Libby scrunched her eyes shut. She had spoken without thinking. The words were true, but after this afternoon, she wasn't at all certain whether he still cared for her beyond friendship.

"Nor you to me, Libby." He took her hand and drew it threw his arm. Her heart began beating erratically.

"Will I find Daniel on your porch this evening, Libby?"

"I hardly think so." The cool evening air didn't keep her cheeks from burning at the memory of the numerous times she'd forgotten or been late for evenings with Pastor Green because she had been with Spencer.

"He's a good man, Libby."

"So you've said before." She snatched her arm back. Just because he might not want her himself didn't give him the right to push her off on someone else. "I do wish people would stop trying to shove men at me. I'm perfectly capable of deciding for myself whether to have a man in my life, and if so, whom."

"Of course, you are." His voice sounded shocked. "It's just that Daniel is a good man and—"

"Ooooh!" Her hands formed into fists at her sides.

"He is. You two have so much in common. How could you help but be happy with him?"

Libby stamped her foot and whirled to face him. "It would help if I loved him. Maybe you think I'm too old for that to matter. Lots of people think so. Well, I don't. I can support myself and take care of my home by myself. I don't need a man around unless I love him."

Spencer chuckled and held up his hands in a gesture of surrender. "All right, all right. It's just that you've always believed it so important that the man you marry shares your faith, and Daniel certainly does."

Frustration ran through her with all the turbulence of the Mississippi in flood season. She wanted to tell him that he was the man she loved, he was the man she wanted to marry, but silly convention didn't allow a woman such freedom. "Pastor Green isn't the only man who shares my faith. It would be a mighty small religion if he were."

Spencer guffawed. "That it would."

Libby started down the sidewalk, her heels sounding smartly against the boards.

Spencer hurried after her, grasping one of her shoulders. "Hold up. What's going on, Libby?"

She swung her arms out from her sides, her drawstring purse swinging wildly. "Why didn't you just tell me that you had asked God into your life? Why did I have to find it out almost by accident?"

"Is that what this is all about?"

She looked down at the pointed toes of her Sunday slippers, not willing to look him in the eye or let him see what was in her eyes.

"Libby, I didn't tell you because I was afraid you wouldn't believe me."

Her head jerked up. "Of course, I would have believed you!"

"Are you sure? You knew I was trying to win your hand, and you'd told me in no uncertain terms more than once that the only way you would marry me is if I shared your faith."

"That's why I don't understand why you didn't tell me. It was the only thing standing between us. Then when the barrier was gone, and you didn't tell me, I thought. . .I was afraid. . ."

"Afraid of what?" His voice held that gentle quality that always unglued her.

She focused on his chest, the top button on his jacket, unable to look him in the face. "I'm afraid you've discovered you don't love me after all." The words were almost a whisper. Then, to her horror, she broke into quiet sobs.

"Ah, Libby, my dearest love." She allowed him to pull her gently against his chest. He wrapped his arms around her, and she buried her face in the wool of his jacket. "I thought I must live my faith for a while before you would believe in my change of heart. Then, too, after I faced the fact that I need God and spent more time reading the Bible, I began to see my past in a different light and saw how cruelly I'd treated you."

"You were never cruel!" Sniff.

"But I was. For years, I've felt sorry for myself. I thought you couldn't have loved me as much as I loved you, or you wouldn't have let anything stand in the way of our life together. I blamed God and your stubbornness and my drinking for the fact that we weren't together. It never occurred to me that I was the one who had abandoned you, abandoned us, abandoned the possibility of a life together. I was the one who was too stubborn to consider turning to God, even to the point of asking Him to show me whether or not He existed or loved me."

Libby wiped a tear from her cheek, hiccuping as her sobs dwindled. A gentle peace filled her breast. She had never thought he would talk like this with her about the struggles with his heart and his faith. His sharing made her feel closer to him than ever before.

"I never *blamed* you for not believing." She sought for the words to explain. "As much as I wanted you to know the joy of trusting Jesus, I always knew you couldn't do it just for me. Your heart wasn't ready to trust Him back then."

"I threw up so many roadblocks." His chest lifted in a deep sigh beneath her cheek. "Even if I wasn't ready to believe in Him, I could have ended our relationship in a kinder way. As you well know, the whole town soon knew the story of my elopement with Margaret. I was so concerned with my own anger and embarrassment that I never realized how abandoned and humiliated you must have felt in front of your family and the town."

Tears welled up again, but this time they were tears of release and gratitude. She hadn't allowed herself to realize how important it was to her that he understand how much he'd hurt her when he married Margaret all those years ago without even a good-bye to her.

"And I thought, I was afraid. . . ," she could hear the amusement creeping into his voice as he repeated her earlier words, "that it wasn't fair to try to steal your heart from a man like Daniel, who would be so good to you and had, like you, loved the Lord most of his life."

"You can't steal my heart from a man who doesn't have it." Her sobs were subsiding, but her voice still shook from them.

"I guess I can't at that." He slipped a knuckle under her chin and lifted her face. He searched her eyes. "Do I need to steal your heart from anyone, or is it already mine?"

Joy-filled peace fell like a mantle on her heart. "It is yours, Spencer. It is yours."

He lowered his face toward hers. A heartbeat away from her lips he whispered, "I love you. I'll always love you."

His lips were tender, as if in awe of the gift life had finally brought him. She lost herself in his kiss, surrendering to the joy of love brought full circle from its youthful beginning.

"Harumph! Such behavior! On a public sidewalk."

Startled, Libby and Spencer jumped apart.

Judge Keyes and his wife were walking past. Mrs. Keyes's distinguished face was filled with indignation.

Libby caught back a giggle, remembering Mrs. Keyes's

nosey questions in her millinery shop as she attempted to ferret out the direction of Libby's affections. She was sorely tempted to stop the woman and tell her, "I choose this one." *But Spencer hasn't actually asked me to marry him, not since he became a believer,* she reminded herself.

Spencer drew her arm through his once more. "Think that swing on your front porch is available? I plan to kiss you at least a few more times before we part tonight, and I'd hate to offend any more of the town's ladies when I do." His eyes twinkled in the glow from gas streetlights.

On the swing, hidden from curious eyes by the spirea bushes planted about the porch, Libby rested contentedly against his shoulder. Mellow light from the lamp in the parlor window allowed her to see the face that was so dear to her. Spencer had kept his word, and she'd been thoroughly kissed.

The dear little hat whose pin had saved the day rested alone at one end of the swing. Spencer's beard caught in Libby's curls as he moved his chin against her hair. She liked the feel of it.

"Ah, Libby, the wonder of being with you after all these years—it's like a miracle. I've imagined it many times, but it was never this sweet in my dreams." His lips touched her hair in a kiss, then the edge of her eyebrow, and the bridge of her nose. "Will you marry me, Libby?"

Libby closed her eyes and let the joy spill over her. "Yes! Oh, yes! In my heart, I'm already married to you."

His arms tightened, and she heard him sigh with love and contentment. "I feel the same way, but I want us to be married in the eyes of God and the world."

"I want that, too." She slid her fingertips over his cheek and looked into his radiant eyes. "I can't think of anything I want more than to spend the rest of our years together as man and wife."

They were silent for awhile, content to hold each other and revel in the wonder of their love. Spencer traced the line of her lips lightly with the tip of his index finger. "What are you thinking that brought that smile, my love?"

"I was remembering the Bible verse I hung onto while trying to learn to live without the hope we would one day be us. 'I waited patiently for the Lord; and he inclined unto me, and heard my cry.' I didn't wait so patiently, but He heard my heart's cry for you anyway."

epilogue

Jennie Lee's dining and social hall shimmered with golden light. It shone from her crystal chandeliers, the brass-trimmed wall sconces, and candles within hurricane holders on the linen-covered tables. It sparkled off the crystal and silver at the place settings. Gold and ivory wallpaper and gold valances above lake-blue velvet draperies intensified the mellow light. Violin music added to the atmosphere the decorating created, and a background to the murmur of the wedding reception crowd milling about the room in the manner of the many crowds who had filled the salon during *Jennie Lee*'s early days.

"You've done a beautiful job on this room, Libby." Constance's gaze wandered over the room.

"Didn't she?" Spencer slipped his arm around Libby's shoulders and gave her a squeeze. "It's elegant yet lighter than most I've seen, and I've seen a number."

Libby slipped a hand over Spencer's and smiled at him, then at Constance. Pleasure at the sincere admiration of two of her favorite people warmed her. As Constance was well aware, she'd used the colors of Constance's parlor as inspiration for the salon.

"When Spencer told me his intention to have the remodeling completed in three months, I didn't think it possible," Libby told Constance, "but with his business connections, he was able to arrange for all the help we needed."

"The room pales next to my bride, don't you think?" Spencer beamed.

"I do, indeed."

Libby ducked her head self-consciously, running the palm of her hand over the embossed satin of her wedding suit. It was quite simple, but elegant. She'd had Ida and Constance's

169

assurance that it did not look too much like a wedding gown to be a proper outfit for a second wedding and a fifty-five-year-old bride. She loved the cream color, the leg-o'-mutton sleeves, the high collar, and dainty pearl trim on the jacket.

She still had no illusions about her beauty. She hadn't been born with a face that would launch a thousand ships and certainly hadn't grown into one through the years. Yet when she looked into Spencer's eyes and saw his love for her reflected there, she felt beautiful. She understood now that he didn't love her looks, he loved the essence of who she was, as she loved him.

"Captain and Mrs. Spencer Matthews." A smiling Pastor Green stopped before them, with Ida beside him. He and Spencer shook hands. "You've a fine wife there, Captain, and she has a fine husband."

"Thank you, Daniel. That means a lot, coming from you. Time was, I thought it would be you standing in this place today."

Libby's cheeks warmed. Her glance went to the toes of her satin shoes, which peeked out from beneath her skirt.

"You have my sincere wish for your happiness." Daniel turned to Ida and raised an eyebrow. "Do you want to tell them, or shall I?"

Ida's smile made little round balls of her cheeks. Her eyes sparkled. "We're getting married. He asked me last night, after your rehearsal."

Libby threw her arms around Ida's neck. "Oh, Ida, I'm so happy for you!" They drew apart, and she looked at Pastor Green with a laugh. "And for you, too, of course."

"I've you to thank for Ida, you know." Pastor Green's eyes twinkled.

"Me?" Libby laid a hand on her chest, surprised.

"Yes, you. If you hadn't stood me up so many times while seeing the captain, I might never have become so well acquainted with Ida."

The laugh the four of them shared was interrupted by Effie and Evan and Spencer's grandsons, two towheaded boys of five and six, as the children pushed in front of Libby and Spencer.

Effie threw herself against Spencer. "We told Lewis and Frank that we helped catch thieves who wanted the dead captain's gold, but they wouldn't believe us."

"Tell them it's true, Captain," Evan urged.

Spencer nodded at his grandsons. "It certainly is true."

The oldest of the boys crossed his arms over his chest. "I won't believe it until I see the treasure."

Effie rolled her eyes in exasperation. "They didn't find the treasure. But Evan and me are going to keep looking for it."

Evan nodded vigorously.

"Oh, dear." Constance's shoulders drooped. "Here we go again."

Spencer shook his head. "I'm afraid that treasure, if it ever existed, is gone for good. It's part of the legends of the Big Muddy, now."

"Maybe not." Effie didn't give up hope so easily.

The youngest boy turned large blue eyes to Spencer. "Did ghosts really try to find the treasure, Grandfather?"

"Of course not," Effie answered before Spencer could respond. "I told you, people only thought there were ghosts. There's no such thing as ghosts. You'll know that when you're older, like me and Evan. Real people tried to find the treasure."

The boy looked disappointed.

Evan turned to the boys. "Want to see the pilothouse? Come on!"

The four raced through the crowd.

Spencer's arm drew Libby close. His whisper in her ear sent delightful chills through her. "I thought my treasure had been lost for good, too. Now that I've found it, I'll never let it go."

"I didn't realize 'never' was such a wonderful word." She whispered, well aware of the crowd about them.

He chuckled.

"I'm glad your sons and their families came for the wedding,

Spencer. I was so afraid they wouldn't want you to remarry."

"They only want me to be happy. They'll love you when they get to know you."

They'd have time to get to know each other. For a wedding trip, Spencer and Libby were taking the *Jennie Lee* to St. Louis. His sons' families and the Knights would be traveling with them.

He took her hand. "Let's go outside. There's something I want to show you."

It took them a long time to work their way through their friends and family to the deck. He led her up the stairs to the texas, then to the front of that level. His arms slid about her shoulders from behind, drawing her back against him. She rested there contentedly.

"I used to imagine how wonderful it would be," he murmured in her ear, "if you wore my name, and everyone would know by my name that you were my wife. But lately, I've been wishing tradition allowed a man to carry his wife's name, also, to show the world her heart belongs to him. I think I've found a way to tell the world you love me. What do you think?"

He pointed toward the pilothouse. Her gaze followed.

She gasped. Tears welled up in her eyes. Above the front windows, in large bold letters, a new name had been painted. *The Lovely Libby*. Her voice trembled as she read the words.

"I renamed the boat. Do you mind?"

"Mind? I think it's the nicest wedding gift any bride has ever received."

His lips touched her neck just below her ear. "Then perhaps you'd like to thank me properly."

"Why, Captain!" Her laugh trembled as she turned in his arms and raised her lips for his kiss. His mouth claimed hers with a passion that took her breath.

Giggles from above barely made their way through her consciousness.

"Libby and the captain, sitting in a tree, k-i-s-s-i-n-g!"

Libby jumped back as far as Spencer's arms allowed. "The

children!" She whirled around, Spencer's chuckle sounding behind her.

Effie and Evan hung out of the pilothouse window, with Spencer's grandchildren beside them. Effie waved. "We're teaching Lewis and Frank detecting!"

"Oh, my!" Libby waved back weakly. "This is going to be quite a voyage, Spencer."

"Quite." Amusement filled the one word. His arms drew her back against him once more.

"No telling what Effie and Evan will lead your grandsons into."

Spencer stilled. He lifted his gaze to the pilothouse and groaned. "Oh, my!"

With a low laugh, Libby turned and slipped her arms around his neck. "Welcome to my world, Captain."

Hearts♥ng Presents
Love Stories Are Rated G!

That's for godly, gratifying, and of course, great! If you love a thrilling love story, but don't appreciate the sordidness of some popular paperback romances, **Heartsong Presents** is for you. In fact, **Heartsong Presents** is the *only inspirational romance book club*, the only one featuring love stories where Christian faith is the primary ingredient in a marriage relationship.

Sign up today to receive your first set of four, never before published Christian romances. Send no money now; you will receive a bill with the first shipment. You may cancel at any time without obligation, and if you aren't completely satisfied with any selection, you may return the books for an immediate refund!

Imagine. . .four new romances every four weeks—two historical, two contemporary—with men and women like you who long to meet the one God has chosen as the love of their lives. . .all for the low price of $9.97 postpaid.

To join, simply complete the coupon below and mail to the address provided. **Heartsong Presents** romances are rated G for another reason: They'll arrive *Godspeed!*

A Letter To Our Readers

Dear Reader:

In order that we might better contribute to your reading enjoyment, we would appreciate your taking a few minutes to respond to the following questions. We welcome your comments and read each form and letter we receive. When completed, please return to the following:

Rebecca Germany, Fiction Editor
Heartsong Presents
PO Box 719
Uhrichsville, Ohio 44683

1. Did you enjoy reading *A Man for Libby*?
   ☐ Very much. I would like to see more books
       by this author!
   ☐ Moderately
       I would have enjoyed it more if _____

       _____._____

       _____

2. Are you a member of **Heartsong Presents**? Yes ☐ No ☐
   If no, where did you purchase this book? _____

   _____

3. How would you rate, on a scale from 1 (poor) to 5 (superior), the cover design? _____

4. On a scale from 1 (poor) to 10 (superior), please rate the following elements.

   _____ Heroine   _____ Plot

   _____ Hero   _____ Inspirational theme

   _____ Setting   _____ Secondary characters

5. These characters were special because_____
_____
_____

6. How has this book inspired your life?_____
_____
_____

7. What settings would you like to see covered in future **Heartsong Presents** books?_____
_____
_____

8. What are some inspirational themes you would like to see treated in future books?_____
_____
_____

9. Would you be interested in reading other **Heartsong Presents** titles? Yes ☐ No ☐

10. Please check your age range:
☐ Under 18 ☐ 18-24 ☐ 25-34
☐ 35-45 ☐ 46-55 ☐ Over 55

11. How many hours per week do you read?_____

Name _____

Occupation _____

Address _____

City _____ State _____ Zip _____